LUKE TELEPHONED several times during his father's week of suspension. Betty refused to talk to him. Knowing her routine rather well, Luke waylaid her on Thursday evening in town as Betty was ambling by City Hall, en route to the public library. Betty grinned and waved amiably, but cold bloodedly beat him to the punch. "I won't discuss your father," she announced. "It's a security matter, period."

"Why are you doing this?" Luke asked hoarsely. "You know what it means, what it must mean."

There was no doubt that Luke had been deeply hurt. His pallid face looked pinched, and there were dark semicircles under his eyes.

Luke gripped her arm. His stubby fingers hurt, but pride prevented Betty from crying out. She met his gray eyes foursquare and said bluntly: "Luke, it would cost me my job to discuss the matter with you. Surely you can understand there are times when one must hold her tongue?"

Without a word, Luke whirled and went across the road to his car.

Was she to lose the man she loved over a matter of principle?

The Questing Heart

A love story by Joan Garrison

The Complete Edition

BELMONT BOOKS • NEW YORK CITY

THE QUESTING HEART

A BELMONT BOOK—MAY 1966
Published originally in
hardcover by Arcadia House

Belmont Productions, Inc.
1116 First Avenue
New York, New York 10021

© 1962 by Arcadia House

PRINTED IN THE UNITED STATES OF AMERICA

Also by Joan Garrison

THE LOVING HEART
B50-638   50¢

SNATCH A DREAM
B50-654   50¢

The Questing Heart

1

It was a lonely, uneventful patrol until shortly after ten o'clock. Bored by the scenery and herself, Betty Sanderson decided it would be the last patrol she would ever walk even if the decision cost her sixty-two hundred dollars a year. Then the ten o'clock whistle blew, and a few minutes later a jeep containing two fellows approached the fence from the rangeland side of the missile test and development center. The fellows didn't spot her, probably because her forest-green uniform blended effectively with the scrub vegetation. The driver halted the jeep about a dozen feet from the fence, and his companion hopped out promptly with a shovel. The fellows apparently hoped to dig their way under the fence and then work their way north to the little hill overlooking the Surface-Launch Building. The bigger fellow was loudly positive they'd get all the motion pictures and stills they wanted from that hilltop. "Boy," he said at least three times in two minutes, "if we make it to that hill we get the newspaper yarn of the year."

Betty wrestled with her conscience.

She lost.

Having lost, she settled down behind a clump of blue-green sage and drew her service revolver from its holster. She had to wait approximately ten minutes. Although the fellows were industrious, they were poor hands with a shovel. Moreover, it was just their luck to hit rock about a foot down, and they had to start all over again somewhere else. Winded by the time they'd gotten under the fence, the fellows decided they could risk cigarettes on the grounds that only coyotes were around to see the smoke. But eventually they came past the clump of sage, muttering and sputtering as they crawled along under the weight of their photographic equipment. Grinning, deciding that she did so have a future as a security agent, Betty rose soundlessly and walked along after them.

It was the bigger fellow who spotted her first. Sweating and blowing, he stopped to rest. He looked back, blinked, and looked again.

"It happens this way," Betty assured him. "The revolver is real, incidentally. My boss says that when I pull the trigger this revolver will go bang and one Russian spy will die under the lovely blue sky of Wyoming. Care to charge me?"

The smaller fellow looked at his companion and said: "You and your big ideas. Look, Leo, next time you get a big idea, will you kindly not clue me in?"

The man named Leo was equal to the occasion, or so he thought. His right hand moved lightning fast. A big handful of sand and alkali came streaking through the air, and Leo yelled: "Run!"

The smaller man didn't run. And Leo, of course, stopped running when he noticed the sand had missed Betty's eyes by about five or six yards.

"Reporters," Leo explained. "Look; let me show you our press cards."

Betty suggested that Leo sit down.

Leo sat down.

"Do you know the difference between a good security agent and a poor one?" Betty asked. "It's the difference between knowing when to shoot and not to shoot. The next time you move, I shoot."

"We're with the *New York Recorder*," the smaller man said. "I'm James Bartlett, and this is Leo Molinaro. You may not believe this, miss, but our assignment is to find out how well these missile test and development centers are guarded. Call our editor if you don't believe me."

Betty worked her walkie-talkie and announced with studied calm: "Sanderson here in zone 3 with two captured invaders."

Muggins said: *"Huh?"*

Betty switched off the walkie-talkie and sat down on a convenient rock. "This will take time," she said easily. "If you fellows want to smoke, go ahead."

Bartlett lighted up, but not big Leo. Leo's brain had finally come abreast of the event. "How come you had us cold pigeon like that?" he asked. "I'd have seen you if you'd just happened along. What you were doing, lady, was waiting for us."

"Not to be impertinent," Betty said, "but you talk too much, sir. Specifically, you talked too much in Ma Hopper's greasy spoon on Central Street the night before last. Ma told me, I told the boss, the boss told me I was crazy, and he stuck me out here to teach me not to believe every rumor I hear."

In the distance, a siren wailed. To Betty, the wails were delightful sounds, but she didn't permit them to distract her attention from the hands of the two men. She knew that if she were in their position she'd do almost anything she could to get on the other side of the fence before reinforcements arrived. Her watchfulness paid off. Just as big Leo jumped to his feet she pulled the trigger of her revolver. The slug spanged from the rock she'd aimed at, and Leo never did move toward the fence. Ashen, his Adam's apple bobbing, he stared at the unwavering revolver. "We're trained carefully by experts," Betty informed him. "Actually, sir, I could easily have shattered one of your kneecaps. Why be silly? It's improbable you'll even go to jail overnight. You tried, you failed, and I'm sure your editor will understand. In fact, I think your editor will be glad you did fail. If a story is important, the security of our country is more important. You see?"

"Leo," Bartlett said, "if you clown around any more I'll help the kid clobber you. Speaking for myself, I'm glad to see with my own eyes that a foreign agent would have a rough time getting secrets out of this place."

The siren wails rose to a shrill cacophony. Not one, but five patrol cars came zeroing in from different angles of the test range. Fully twenty men came charging from the cars, guns drawn, to surround the area in approved fashion. The chief security officer himself barked an order, and all the men moved in as if to take an enemy strong point by storm. The poor newspaper men were knocked flat and then manacled and searched. A couple of minutes later they were being whisked away in one of the patrol cars, and the other guards were ransacking the area to make certain no one else had sneaked into forbidden territory. The zeal with which the search was conducted amused Chief Hoyt. "Sanderson," he drawled, "take a good close look at some real bloodhounds in action. They can search an area very effectively, can't they, after a cocky brunette has captured the spies for them. Nice work, incidentally. I'm pleased I made no error in assigning you to this key patrol, Sanderson. I'll admit I was nervous when the big idea occurred to me. But you measured up, just as I thought you would. Sanderson, I want to shake your hand."

He shook Betty's hand.

Still, he added, she might as well remain on patrol in zone 3 until lunch. He hoped she didn't mind, but there were things to do. Did she understand?

Meeting his watery gray eyes, Betty said she definitely did understand.

Chief Hoyt was offended. "Sanderson," he said, "I dislike your tone. Your tone insinuates you think I'll go straight to Mr. Abernathy and Dr. Schroeder and steal all the credit for your exploit. Is that what you're thinking?"

With a energetic effort, Betty managed to hold her tongue.

"No such thoughts in my mind," Chief Hoyt said, aggrieved. "It's a matter of record that you apprehended these spies. But there's more to all this than you realize. What you don't know, Sanderson, is that our department has been under fire lately for using what some people have called melodramatic and antiquated methods. I want to get the full story to the ears of the wheels. Then at the strategic time I want to call you into their presence to prove our methods here are so good even a slip of a girl can apply them effectively. Now do you understand?"

Betty said she didn't, and his color went purple-red. He turned and left without another word, and after all the dust stirred up by the patrol cars had settled, Betty resumed her lonely patrol. A half-mile to Gate J, a mile back to Gate K, with walkie-talkie reports to make every fifteen minutes. Then, at eleven-fifteen, in accordance with instructions, she climbed the little hill the reporters had been heading for and scanned the terrain carefully to make certain no one was in the missile area. She gave the all-clear signal to the launch-control officer by radio. He said: "Protect yourself girlie; here comes a DAGGER II!" About five minutes later a couple of jet pursuit aircraft came streaking in from the east. When they were approximately a thousand yards from the Surface-Launch Building the great DAGGER II missile roared up from the launch pad and the jet pilots had to cut in their after-burners to keep up with the sleek flame-orange missile. You could see the missile lurch over into flight attitude as one of the pilots assumed radio command control of the test. A minute later the missile and accompanying jet aircraft were out of sight and the first flight test of the DAGGER II surface-to-surface missile was history.

History made without benefit of newspaper coverage, Betty exulted.

At noon, when she was relieved, she retained possession of her service revolver. Fred Teller gave her a sidelong glance as he headed the patrol car for the Security Building. "Feeling your oats?" Fred asked. "You know the rules, honey. Hand the artillery over, please."

"I'd love to frame it, Fred. Woman and girl, I've never shot a finer revolver. The big fellow, Leo Molinaro, tried to make a run for it. He stopped running, though, when I hit the three-inch rock I was aiming at. Fred, I could win a marksmanship prize with this revolver."

He kept his right hand out, however, and she finally unloaded the revolver and gave it to him. After that, Fred became his naturally amiable self. "Good job, honey. You should have seen the chief's face when Muggins gave him your news. The chief turned green. I never saw a man look so sick so fast in my life. By the way, the fellows *are* reporters. That was the first thing Mr. Abernathy himself had checked."

Betty started to laugh, but a thought sent a chill through her. "We were lucky, Fred, do you know that? It was a clever plan. We don't patrol that area as completely as we should. The fact they were able to drive unobserved across that range proves that. Suppose Ma Hooper hadn't overheard their talk in her restaurant. Right now there'd be some embarrassing pictures for the King Abernathy Corporation to explain to the Department of Defense."

Fred nodded, his gray hair flashing like silver in the March sunshine. "That's what made the chief turn so sick so fast, honey. Want a promotion?"

"Yup."

"The chief and I had a fast powwow during the ride back after the prisoners. He made no promises, you understand, but he sort of implied he might be able to give you a department to watchdog if you cooperated with him now."

"Can do; will do."

Fred met Betty's twinkling brown eyes and scowled. "Apparently you were expecting him to offer you a deal. Where does a nice girl like you get so many crafty ideas from? Hang it, honey, it's plain incongruous."

"Very simple, Fred. My mother would like to be mistress of the Jolly S Ranch again. The more money I earn, the sooner I can buy it for her."

"All you have to do is marry Pritchard. You know what about Pritchard? The rumor is that he's the next head of the Laboratory Evaluation Department.

A man earning eighteen thousand a year can afford to buy a two-bit ranch like that."

"But if a girl happens to love a small-town doctor?"

Fred's lips were compressed into a thin line. Knowing his opinion of Dr. Luke Masters, Betty changed the subject hurriedly.

"Message for the chief," she said. "I'd love to be security agent in the Technical Information Department. The pay is seven thousand a year, and the people there are interesting."

"We thought Supply and Fiscal would be nice, honey. Look, just between you and me, Tech Info is a rough place to work and it'll get rougher."

"That's what I thought. If a girl did a good job in a rough department she'd naturally be worth more to the corporation. When I'm earning about eight thousand a year I'll be able to buy the Jolly S."

A queer thing happened.

"Don't demand it," Fred ordered. "You hear? Don't demand it!"

Then Fred snapped his mouth shut with the uncomfortable expression of a top security agent who knew that he'd said too much.

2

THE MESSAGE dutifully carried to Chief Hoyt by Fred Teller was apparently considered to be satisfactory. Shortly after lunch, Betty received an invitation to discuss her exploit with Mr. Thomas R. Quigley, the industrial relations officer. He received her affably in his sunlit office, chuckling wrinkles into his red, fleshy face as she took the indicated green leather chair. "You surprised me, Miss Sanderson," he announced. "I was prepared to see an Amazon. How much do you weigh?"

"Approximately a hundred and twelve pounds, sir."

"Yet you made those two fellows believe you were practically an army! A remarkable performance, Miss Sanderson. You have every reason to feel proud of yourself."

For the second time that day, Betty wrestled with her conscience. This time, however, she won. "It wasn't a remarkable performance, sir," she contradicted him softly. "I happened to be in the right spot at the right time. If you're armed and know how to shoot, it's quite easy to control such a situation."

"All in a day's work, eh?"

"Nor were they even professional spies, sir—men trained to make a good fight until the last. The big fellow had spirit but no know-how. I knew it, so I had the psychological edge, plus the advantage of the loaded artillery."

"How did you just happen to be in the right place at the right time, Miss Sanderson? It could hardly have been coincidental. That fence is approximately three miles long, yet they made their penetration between Gates J and K and you just happened to be waiting between Gates J and K."

Betty gave him the full story. His grizzled brows lifted once or twice, and then, quite happily, he jotted down the address of Ma Hooper's restaurant in town. "This delights me," he said. "Public relations is part of my job here, Miss Sanderson. New York headquarters deems it essential that we enjoy good relations with the community. The fact that this Mrs. Hooper passed the information along to you indicates the community is both loyal to our country and friendly with this division of the corporation. New York will be pleased to know that."

"Well, we are Americans here in Wyoming, sir. And why shouldn't we feel well disposed toward a company that has given many of us the best jobs of our lives?"

He was surprised. "Home town talent, then, Miss Sanderson?"

"Born in Antelope View, sir, and raised here."

"Ranch girl?"

Betty nodded. It occurred to her suddenly that he was asking these questions not because he didn't have the answers in his file cabinet but because he wanted an opportunity to study her, appraise her. She wondered what job, if any, he was considering her for.

She decided that while she really wanted to watch dog the Technical Information Department, she would grab any other department that was offered, even Supply and Fiscal.

Mr. Quigley said with elaborate casualness: "I understand that ranch people are expert in the art of saying little, Miss Sanderson. I wonder if that's true in your particular case. Let me be frank with you. You are here for two reasons. The first reason is that I want to impress upon you the fact there must be no publicity whatsoever concerning your adventure this morning. The whole matter will be settled in New York. Have you discussed the affair with anyone?"

"Just security people, sir."

"Fine. Keep it that way. If anyone asks you questions, simply say the whole thing was a misunderstanding, that the men were authorized visitors who had mislaid their identification badges. All right?"

"Certainly, sir."

Mr. Quigley stood up and looked at his wristwatch. He shrugged. "As for the second reason I brought you here, Miss Sanderson: quite simply, I wanted to determine for myself if you're as level-headed as Chief Hoyt claims you are. You've passed the test, if that's the word for it. Now, then, will you be kind to a man who appreciates your skill and courage and wants to help you get ahead? Just don't become a rattlebrain the instant you reach the Technical Information Department. Mr. Herman and I have been at loggerheads for years. I certainly don't want to give him an opportunity to say I goofed when I made you security agent for his department."

For a moment, Betty could not believe her ears. He understood, and he reached out and patted her shoulder quite paternally. "Ah," he said gruffly, "you've certainly earned a chance, Miss Sanderson. In fact, if I had my way, I'd have you honored properly in our auditorium. The truth your modesty prevented you from divulging is that you *couldn't* be sure those men were just reporters. Mr. Calvin Abernathy and Dr. Schroeder admire you, Miss Sanderson, just as I do. For political reasons you won't be honored publicly, but you're certainly going to be given every chance to work as a senior security agent in the field. If Herman gives you any problems, let me know directly."

Feeling dazed, feeling giddy with excitement, Betty managed to blurt out thank you's of a kind and get back to her cubby-hole office in the Security Building without disgracing herself. There, however, where she could be herself, she let out a girlish "Yippee!" that brought Elaine Muggins in from the nearby communications room. The plump redhead looked her over suspiciously and asked: "Are you feeling a reaction to that strain this morning? Chief Hoyt says he doesn't understand why you haven't had a severe reaction."

Betty grabbed her telephone.

"Honey," Elaine said, "how can I connect you with a party when I'm here? Look, perhaps you ought to go over to the medical office for a checkup."

"I demand Chief Hoyt!"

Elaine raised her arms and flapped them like wings. "En route to New York, honey, with two visitors who happened to mislay their identification badges. Who are they all trying to kid?"

"Where's Fred Teller, then?"

Elaine shrugged. "Out cussing somewhere, I imagine. Just after you left to see Mr. Quigley, Fred was told to transfer you to Tech Info forthwith. Fred blew his stack. There's a jeep waiting for you in the parking lot, and you're to drive over to Tech Info whenever you wish. Fred gave me one other message for you. 'Red,' he told me, 'you tell the brunette she's flipped.' So I'm telling you that you've flipped.' "

Betty pronged the handset, scooped up her handbag and headed for the parking lot. Ten minutes later she had the intense satisfaction of announcing in the reception room of the Technical Information Department that she was the department's new security agent. The receptionist laughed. "Honey," she said, "jokes like that aren't considered funny around here. We don't have security agents. Mr. Herman eats them for breakfast."

"Speaking of whom, may I see him?"

The receptionist nipped into a nearby office and returned with a woman she introduced as Marge Abern. Marge was Mr. Harold Herman's secretary, and Marge was better informed than the receptionist. "We've been expecting you," Marge said cheerfully. She held out her hand. "Welcome to Tech Info, Miss Sanderson. I imagine the print shop crew will be pleased."

"Right now, no," Betty said dolefully. "I had Mr. Masters to dinner last night, and he found the roast beef too rare. Mr. Masters never forgives such crimes."

Grinning, Marge led her along a short hall and rapped softly on Mr. Herman's door. Mr. Herman rose as they entered and smiled genially as Marge made both the introduction and announcement. "My," he twitted her, "the news a department head is always the last to receive. Do sit down, Betty. May I call you Betty? I'd suggest a cup of coffee, but I'm scheduled for an urgent conference in ten minutes."

"Seven minutes, sir," Marge said. "And will you be

certain, sir, to take the DAGGER III graphics up to the conference? Dr. Schroeder is most anxious to review them."

He nodded, and waved Marge out.

"The good Lord deliver you from an efficient secretary." He laughed. "But I imagine the department would be one vast administrative snarl if it weren't for Marge's efficiency."

His brown eyes, however, were not laughing. It was clear that Mr. Harold Herman had received an unanticipated jolt and that he resented it.

"Been here long?" he asked mildly. "I don't recall having met you before, Miss Sanderson."

"Three years, sir. I came here directly from college. Chief Hoyt selected me from the steno pool when his secretary resigned to marry. Then they developed a requirement for a girl who could function as security agent on occasion. One thing led to another, and last year I was made full-time security agent."

"Rather interesting, that. I thought Chief Hoyt had a dim opinion of women in general."

"He may have, sir, I wouldn't know. I do know, however, that he's been a good man to work for. Take this assignment, for example. I'm sure Chief Hoyt could have blocked it had he wanted to."

Mr. Harold Herman picked up a pencil and began to doodle on a scrap of notepaper. "Precisely what is your assignment here, Miss Sanderson? Are you to conduct regular security checks; are you to insure we obey all security regulations; are you to read all material to make certain that secret information isn't published in a confidential report, say? I'm quite annoyed with Mr. Quigley. I really think all this should have been discussed with me before you were sent over."

"I would imagine, sir," Betty said carefully, "that I'm to do whatever other agents do elsewhere. I haven't been given detailed instructions because Chief Hoyt had to make a flight to New York. Until he returns I'll just play it by ear, familiarize myself with your department, check the personnel records, and so forth."

"Did Mr. Quigley say if this assignment has been cleared with Mr. Abernathy and Dr. Schroeder? I'd be surprised if it has. You see, Miss Sanderson, ours is a rather unique department. We develop no information. We merely process that information for dissemination to authorized people. And artists and writers and motion picture people aren't easily regimented, you know. Dr. Schroeder in particular has always been aware of our special problems, and he has always been inclined to allow us to handle our security problems in our own way."

"I believe the assignment was cleared with Mr. Abernathy and Dr. Schroeder, sir."

Mr. Herman let his breath out in a long sigh. "Now I wonder why?" he asked. "Surely there haven't been any leaks, Miss Sanderson?"

"I wouldn't know, sir."

"And wouldn't tell me if you did?"

"And wouldn't tell you if I did, sir. I operate under orders to watch and listen but talk little."

Knuckles rapped the door. Marge Abern came in, looking disturbed. "Mr. Herman," she said, "you'll be late. Really, sir, this is a most important conference!"

He said testily: "Calm down, Marge, and take a memo for immediate dispatch to Mr. Quigley."

His secretary rolled her eyes but got her notebook and pencil.

Looking straight at Betty, his brown eyes narrowed and hard, the Technical Information officer dictated: "I wish to protest the assignment of Miss Elizabeth Sanderson to the post of security agent for this department. The assignment was made prior to discussion with me. I do not know why Miss Sanderson has been sent to us, I do not know what her duties are to be, and I do not even know if a girl of her years and education is qualified to function in an environment as highly technical as ours. I therefore propose to argue this matter with the highest authorities, my objective being to secure the instant return of Miss Sanderson to the security office."

Mr. Herman popped up from his chair, a dapper man with a balding head and a most engaging smile. "Nothing personal in this," he assured Betty. "One of these evenings you must allow me to prove that by taking you to dinner. Now, girls, if you'll excuse me?"

There was a long silence after he'd left. Then Marge Abern said loyally: "You'll learn to love him, Miss Sanderson. He just likes action, that's all."

3

Dr. Luke Masters was properly impressed when Betty told him of her promotion during their customary Sunday flapjack breakfast. "It could be," he said dryly, "that you have a talent for security work." His clear gray eyes said infinitely more, and in the saying brought a blush to Betty's cheeks. Made somewhat emotional by his eloquent eyes, she proceeded to do the one thing she had vowed three months ago she would never do again. "Good sir," she said, "may I propose marriage? With my fat pay check week I thee endow."

"You'd better be careful," he warned. "This wasn't my most profitable week. I may surprise you one of these days and accept."

Betty asked frankly: "Why not? You'd not be the first young doctor to get a financial lift from his wife during the early stages of his career. In fact, I once met a girl who worked hard to send her doctor-husband abroad to do some special studying. What matters, really—the source of the income or the marriage relationship?"

Across the range, visible from the kitchen window, came a long line of cattle. They were Wobbly W cattle taking the usual liberties with Jolly S land and grass. It irritated Betty to see them out there, but she knew better than to let the sight spoil her pleasure in the moment. "People are odd," she said lightly. "Calvin Abernathy and his wife own the Wobbly W, meaning there's enough money over there to keep their fences in order. But apparently the rich, like the poor, don't ever object to getting something for nothing."

"What difference does it make if those cattle eat the grass?"

"Property rights ought to be respected, for one thing. For another, I hope to buy this place back from the bank one day. I'd like to have a rich range then on which to run a big herd."

Luke held his empty plate out, and Betty refilled it with flapjacks and sausage. "You should eat more," she said as she always did. "Also, you should give a girl an answer when she proposes."

"When I can afford to support you properly, I'll do the proposing," Luke said. "Until then, please don't tempt me. I'm not made of brass, you know."

Betty wanted to clout him. Yet at the same time she had to admire his determination to succeed on his own.

The ringing telephone interrupted her thoughts. It was Mrs. Calvin Abernathy, her voice worried. "Is Dr. Masters there?" she asked. "His father told me I could reach Dr. Masters at this number. This is Mrs. Calvin Abernathy at the Wobbly W. We need Dr. Masters at once."

Luke hustled off about three minutes later, still chewing pancakes and sausage. When he returned around ten he had an interesting tale to relate. An elderly bronc buster the Abernathys had hired, it seemed, had ridden one bronc too many. The bronc had thrown the fellow in jig time, and the fellow had suffered a fractured hip. "Neck of the femur," Luke elaborated painstakingly. "I doubt he'll ride any more broncs."

Betty drew a deep breath. "Clay Singleton, no doubt?"

"That's the fellow. Why?"

"Used to ride for us, Luke. Right here on the Jolly S. May I go see him?"

"Well, not today. In fact, not for several days. I've suggested that a specialist be called in to set that bone, meaning it won't be set much before tomorrow afternoon."

Betty was puzzled. "Can't you set a bone?"

"Yup. Still, peeling broncs is Clay Singleton's way of earning a living. Why should I jeopardize his career just to pick up a fat fee from the Abernathys? He needs the best there is, and I'm not the best."

"Still . . ."

Luke wagged his glossy black head. "You fell in love with the wrong fellow, I'm afraid. I actually entered this profession to help people, not to make a mint of money. What price ideals!"

A half-hour later the telephono rang again. This time the call was from a fellow with downright panic in his voice. One of his children, he said, had gotten to playing with a hatchet and had chopped off one of his fingers. "Tell Doc the blood is spoutin', will you?" he yelled. "Tell him to come fast."

Betty got the name and address, and this time accompanied Luke in his elderly but quite serviceable Ford. While Luke was busy inside the ranchhouse, the distraught father bemoaned the Porterfield luck on the wooden bench before the dilapidated barn. "Us

Porterfields can't never win," Mr. Porterfield said. "If it ain't one thing it's another. Sometimes I've got a mind just to walk out of here and get as far away as I can get. I keep thinking I could change my luck in California."

"What would your wife and children do?" Betty asked.

"Oh, never you mind about Lucy and the kids," he said. "Don't come much prettier than Lucy. Lucy wouldn't have no trouble finding another husband."

"You must be a big help around the place," Betty told him. "I love the way you maintain this ranch. I haven't seen a more run-down place in my life."

He shot her an irate glance. "Don't put on no airs with me," he said. "I know about you Sandersons. Your father dropped dead one day on account of doing so much work. You're no better off right now than us. Leastwise, we still own our ranch."

Luke came out and smiled reassuringly at Mr. Porterfield. "Cutting a finger isn't the same as chopping one off," he said. "Joe will be all right and he'll keep his finger."

"You think I'm blind, Doc? But the way things are these days, nobody comes to the Porterfields unless a guy screams about an emergency. I sure wish I could pay you, though. Yes, sir, I sure wish that."

Luke's smile never wavered. "The fee is five dollars, Mr. Porterfield. Pay when you can."

The man's eyes narrowed. "What about two dollars right now in cash, Doc? I owe you somethin', I know that. If I could just afford to . . ."

Betty never allowed him to get farther. Having spotted a fine-looking Winchester .22 leaning against the barn wall, she went over and picked up the rifle and grinned amiably at Luke. "This is good security for your fee," she said. "Hock it for five dollars, and send the pawn ticket to Mr. Porterfield."

Mr. Porterfield came up, roaring. "You keep your hands off my property!" he roared. "You want me to call the sheriff?"

Betty tucked the rifle under her arm and went over to Luke's car. "You just go ahead and telephone the sheriff," she said. "The sheriff will be mighty interested in hearing our side of the story."

Mr. Porterfield cussed, the presence of a woman notwithstanding. In the end, however, he handed five one-dollar bills to Luke. Naturally, he then ordered them off·his property and cocked the rifle to prove he meant business.

Five dollars richer, Luke was inclined to be somewhat expansive during the five-mile ride back to Antelope View. "I ought to make you my collection agent," he joshed. "That's my major problem at the moment. I have no difficulty getting clients; just fees."

"You're too soft," Betty told him. "Ideals are fine, but softness isn't. How much are you owed?"

"Oh, a thousand, more or less."

"What do doctors do about fees they can't collect?"

"Eventually, you turn them over to a collection agency in exchange for so much on the dollar. But who wants to deliver people to the tender mercies of a collection agency?"

At that point, Betty began to wish she could point a gun at him and compel him to marry her. The poor wonderful guy needed a keeper, doggone it!

But then Luke turned into Green River Road and it suddenly didn't matter. He followed the road for a mile, then swung left into an earthen road that carried them up among the hills to the site of their future home. His father was there, of course, happily banging nails into the foundation. "Sightseers *ver-*

boten!" George Masters yelled. "Especially lousy cooks."

Betty got out anyway to check on the progress made since last week. "At this rate," she kidded, pleased, "it'll be only five or ten years more, sir. And how come you're using low-grade lumber for the mud-sills of my house?"

Chunky Mr. Masters hefted his hammer and took some short steps forward. "Just say more," he dared. "It must be fun to brain a woman."

During the week since her last visit, Betty saw, he'd just about completed the foundation and he'd brought in a truckload of studs. The studs were fine lumber, kiln-dried, she suspected, and most of them had already been cut to the correct length. Grinning, she took hold of one end of a stud and began to drag it over to the foundation. "Let's put up a few," she suggested. "If Luke and I tote and hold, won't that speed things up a bit?"

"Isn't woman's work, hang it."

"Rubbish, Pop."

"And I'm not your Pop. Not yet, at any rate!"

Betty looked at Luke, and they toted the first stud to the foundation.

Mr. George Masters dropped his hammer. "It's bad enough," he complained, "having you snoop around the print shop all week in Tech Info. I won't have you snooping around here, and that's final. When a fellow builds a fine house for his son, he wants to be left alone."

"And Tech Info wants to be left alone, sir. I know, I know. But that isn't how life is. Take Tech Info, for example. Just for kicks, I called for three secret reports last week. Could they be located? It took almost three hours. In each case, the report in question wasn't even in the custody of the original borrower from the reports library. And would you like to hear more? In all but one case, the original borrower hadn't received a signed slip from the person he passed the report to. I ask you!"

"Can't fiddle round with all that paper work if you want quick production," George Masters argued. "In the print shop alone, all that paper work would cost us maybe ten hours a week."

Betty met his troubled blue eyes.

"Off the record," she said, "most of the offenders are in your group, sir. Say a report just can't be located? Who gets the demerit; who gets fired?"

"Calculated risk, girl!"

"Not any more," Betty told him. "I've sat around for a week in Tech Info, and I've liked little of what I've seen there. As of Monday, security regulations are obeyed, or else."

"For seven thousand a year," he said, "why don't you just sit back and keep quiet and make no enemies? I'd do that if I were you."

"It's my job not to sit back, Pop. Well, do we work or talk?"

"You walk," he ordered, "or you'll build this house yourself."

They did walk. They walked to the rear of the property and down a slope to a pretty stand of pines and a flashing stream. Betty removed her shoes and socks and rolled up her slacks and stuck her feet into the icy water. Luke laughed boyishly and did the same.

"Fine place for our kids," Luke said. "When I was a boy I used to dream of living in a place like this. Interesting, isn't it, how a dream remains with you all your life?"

"Interesting. Wonderful. If you married me now we could sink my income into this place and complete it before autumn. Also, I could scurry around Antelope

View and vicinity and collect those fees for you. And last but not least, I could take Pop under my wing and make certain he doesn't ruin his career."

Luke swung around, concerned. "That security stuff you were discussing is that serious?"

"That serious, Luke. Let me put it this way. When technical information is labeled secret, that information could hurt us if it fell into the wrong hands. They've been lax in your father's print shop at the center. It could be his job. It could also be the end of his government clearance to handle classified information. You see?"

He did, but not for very long. His beautiful brunette beloved smiled, and at long last he leaned forward to kiss her ...

4

Durⁱng his twenty-two year career with the great King Abernathy Corporation, Mr. Harold Herman had learned the wisdom of bending before every administrative storm until he knew exactly how severe the storm was. Typically, therefore, he offered no apparent resistance to the new security agent who had been assigned to his department so arbitrarily by Mr. Quigley. Mr. Herman did see to it that the girl was given the least desirable vacant office. He also saw to it that none of the division and branch heads would make the error of cooperating with her wholeheartedly. But these were routine steps taken to impress upon her the fact that the Technical Information Department had functioned nicely for many years without her and that she really was quite unimportant in the departmental scheme of things. Although it galled Mr. Herman to have in his department an employee not subject to his control, he managed to endure the situation with reasonable equanimity until he learned through Marge Abern that the attractive Miss Sanderson was displeased by the way too many security regulations were honored only in the breach. But once he realized that this particular storm could prove to be most severe indeed, Mr. Herman abandoned passivity for attack.

He began the attack by paying a surprise visit to her office at the far end of the building. He found Miss Sanderson at her desk, a fact he didn't like although he pretended otherwise. "A full day's work for a full day's pay, Miss Sanderson? How refreshing to see someone your age who expects to earn her salary. How do you like your office?"

Her brown eyes flicked to him and then through him, or so it seemed. She asked offhandedly: "Am I really supposed to like it, sir? I thought you'd buried me here to spite Mr. Quigley."

He chuckled and sat down and contrived to pretend he found the low temperature quite comfortable. "I don't know why," he said, "but I thought you would appreciate the quiet and fresh air."

"Well, it doesn't matter, sir," she said. "I discussed the frigidity of this office with Chief Hoyt, and he's promised to mention the matter to Dr. Schroeder."

Mr. Herman forced a laugh. "It must be nice," he said, "to be able to reach the ear of our chief scientist whenever you wish. I must cultivate your friendship, Miss Sanderson. A poor department head never knows when he'll need a friendly ear topside."

She swung around to face him. Her right hand flicked to the left lapel of her forest-green jacket, as if a speck of dust there had troubled her. For the first time, Mr. Herman saw a little blue-and-white ribbon in the lapel buttonhole. For a moment, a moment only, he almost panicked. He managed to say with surface calm, though: "Miss Sanderson, I didn't know you had won our order of merit. How remarkable! As I understand it, only about ten of this corporation's fifty thousand employees have won that ribbon."

"Eight," the girl told him. "So Mr. Abernathy told me last week when he handed it to me in his office."

Mr. Herman stood up briskly. "Miss Sanderson," he said, "allow me to congratulate you, please. Now, then, you must allow me to send the editor of our division newspaper to you. This must be publicized! Fancy a person attached to my department wearing the order of merit! Miss Sanderson, I'm proud to have you in my department."

"Publicity is forbidden, sir," she said crisply. "A security matter was involved, and the matter is still hush-hush. That's why the ribbon was given me privately."

Mr. Herman sat down again, troubled by a nagging thought. "I do wish," he said, "that you had come to me concerning the inadequate heating of this office, Miss Sanderson. You must never assume I'm too busy to concern myself with the welfare of an employee. You see before you, Miss Sanderson, a man who has been through the corporation mill. When I joined this organization twenty-two years ago, I was a very junior technical editor. Our sole plant was in New Jersey, then, and our sole business involved the development of more satisfactory radio broadcasting equipment. As the corporation grew, expanded, my career grew with it. But I've never forgotten what it was like to be a young and very junior technical editor. I always do my best for the young in my department."

Her quirked brunette eyebrows told him her opinion of *that* speech.

Ruffled, Mr. Herman turned to the official reason for the surprise visit he'd paid her. He took the offending memo from his jacket pocket and laid it on her desk. "As a case in point," he said, "notice I'm returning this memo to you rather than turning it over to Mr. Abernathy. Such memos, Miss Sanderson, automatically infuriate department heads. You really have no right to distribute such memos through my department without my authorization to do so. But I come to you with my complaint. Why? Well, as I've said, I've never forgotten what it was like to be a very junior technical editor."

Her stare delighted Mr. Herman. Feeling his first attack had gone off well, he returned to his office and spent a good hour composing a letter of complaint to the general manager. He had the complaint typed in triplicate, and he saw to it that the extra copy was dispatched to Chief Hoyt. Mr. Herman then sat back to wait developments.

Chief Hoyt came over early the next morning. He had the carbon of the complaint with him. "Fine hatchet job, this," he said, laying it on the desk. "Herman, correct me if I'm wrong, but I don't think you love my Betty Sanderson."

"Reasonable complaint, Chief. However, if Mr. Abernathy disagrees with me, I'll withdraw it."

"Oh, the kid was out of line, Herman, no doubt of that. But so what? Why make a big deal out of it? You think you people here never goof? Nuts. I'll bet you a thousand pins to a button that we can prove you people outgoof us. And I kid you not, Herman, believe me."

The Technical Information officer elegantly patted his balding head with his handkerchief. "Could be," he admitted cheerfully. "We'll see. Or would you prefer to trade, Chief?"

"Trade what for what?"

"The complaint will be withdrawn, and your agent will be given every consideration here. In exchange, you tell me exactly why she is here. I don't like the smell of all this, Chief. That girl was sent here before the assignment was discussed with me. In the two weeks she's been here, she's made everyone jumpy by suddenly demanding a sight check of this or that material. What is all this about? Is something missing? Do you suspect one of my employees of being disloyal to our country? That's what I want: information."

"Nuts."

Mr. Herman sighed. He picked up his telephone handset and launched stage two of his attack.

To Lupe Vargas he said: "Lupe, please inform Mr. Abernathy that I must chat with him at once on an urgent and classified matter. I'll hold the line, thank you."

But Chief Hoyt refused to be bluffed. "It's your neck, Herman," he said; "not mine. For old time's sake, I'm returning this carbon to you. And I'll give you some free advice, too. Be smart, shut up, and cooperate fully with Sanderson."

The chunky security officer marched out just as Lupe Vargas announced: "Mr. Abernathy will see you now, Mr. Herman. You may have half an hour."

Harold Herman went first to the men's room, where he carefully washed his face and hands and slicked his few remaining hairs into place. To quiet his nerves, he smoked half a cigarette, being careful to ditch it, of course, in the ash tray on Lupe's desk in the anteroom of Mr. Calvin Abernathy's office. Although it was a difficult feat to perform, Mr. Herman then stepped jauntily into the general manager's office and murmured: "So good of you, sir, to see me so promptly."

The green eyes probed, very sharp eyes that reminded Mr. Herman of the boy's uncle in New York. "I always enjoy seeing you," Calvin Abernathy said, grinning. "Herman, you always make me feel terribly important. Sit down. Smoke, if you wish. I gave it the old college try, as Alice will tell you, but nicotine still holds me in thrall."

Mr. Herman offered him a cigarette, and both lighted up from the same match.

"The Sanderson matter?" Calvin Abernathy asked. He laughed, wagging his red head. "Be careful with that glorious brunette, Herman. I gave her the order of merit, and do you know what she did. She proceeded to scold me for allowing my cattle to forage on Jolly S range. I couldn't say a word. Old Dr. Schroeder had more fun during that ceremony than he's had in years. Don't ever tangle with her, Herman."

Mr. Herman decided this was a warning. He said promptly: "It isn't my ambition to tangle with anyone, sir. Still, I head the department, and it's my job to make sure our work load is handled quickly and effectively. It has occurred to me that I could do a better job if Miss Sanderson were under my direct authority. I could then correlate her important work with the regular work of the department. But if I don't know what her work is, what her requirements are, what her schedule is—well, you see the problem, I'm sure."

"Meaning that in the course of doing her work she prevents your people from doing theirs?"

"Oh, she tries to be reasonable, sir, no doubt of that. The interference with output certainly isn't deliberate. But let me give you an example. As you know, we must process a lengthy electronics countermeasures report each month for the perusal of the Department of Defense. This is a high priority publication. Our deadline can be met, but only by dint of great effort and some overtime. Well, sir, last week everything had to be held in abeyance while the technical editors tried to track down a confidential report that was apparently mislaid a couple of years ago. The report involved the now defunct Abernathy missile checkout system. In other words, whether the report is found or not or whether it falls into Russian hands or not is completely unimportant. Still, work on a high-priority report detailing current work in an extremely important field was held up for two days until it was proven to Miss Sanderson's satisfaction that the missing confidential report was not in the Tech editorial offices. Now, sir, I ask you!"

"Say she was under your authority, Herman. What would you have done?"

"Postponed the search until the high-priority report had been published and distributed."

"And if she were under your authority, Herman, what would you do when she proceeded to investigate you personally and your immediate staff?"

Mr. Herman's jaw dropped.

The long, lean, quite handsome redhead knocked ash from his cigarette. He said slowly, thoughtfully: "I'd better put it this way, Herman. After Miss Sanderson had distinguished herself it was thought to make her security agent for Supply and Fiscal. My uncle was interested in both her physical and mental feats, however, and he teletyped a direct order that she be given the order of merit and assigned to your department. Care to argue with him?"

For the first time in many years, Mr. Harold Herman was shaken. He asked hoarsely: "Then something is wrong in my department? What is it, sir? Why haven't I been told?"

"For the simple reason, Herman, that I haven't been told. Now let me ask you a question. Are you entirely satisfied that every employee in Tech Info scrupulously conforms with every security regulation, minor though that regulation may be?"

"Of course they don't! We live with the regulations

only because we discriminate between the important and the minor. Mr. Abernathy, we handle hundreds of pages of technical information every day. If we signed for this page and that page and entered their numbers in the log books and so forth, we'd never get information processed."

Calvin Abernathy suggested: "Why not allow Miss Sanderson to do the discriminating for you, Herman?"

Mr. Herman drew a deep breath. Then, recognizing that this administrative storm was most severe, he proceeded to bend before it. "Miss Sanderson," he said, "is most welcome in my department, sir. My objections are withdrawn."

5

BETTY was not surprised several days later when she was shifted to a commodious, well-heated, well-lighted, and relative soundproof office at the administrative end of the Technical Information Building. Nor was she surprised when Mr. Herman pronounced her furniture poor and had new furniture shipped over by Supply and Fiscal. What did surprise her, however, was the fear the man manifested in her presence. He behaved for all the world like a man with an uneasy conscience. Her first day in the new office he popped in on her a dozen times, and on each occasion he emphasized his willingness to aid her in whatever way he could. The last time he barged in, he interrupted an interesting conversation she was having with Abner Pritchard. Mr. Herman was distressed. "So sorry," he said earnestly. "Had I known you were busy, Miss Sanderson, I would not have disturbed you."

After he'd left, Betty wagged her head. "Never be a security agent," she warned Abner. "People either hate you or cooperate ad nauseum."

"And Herman does both?"

Betty settled back in her desk chair. She loved her new office and she loved the sensation it gave her to have Abner see her established there, the old flunky days over at last. "He's a man afraid," she said gently. "I can tell you more, I think. He's needlessly afraid. I've often noticed that conscientious and loyal people are usually more afraid of security agents than the out-and-out traitors."

Abner asked: "How many traitors have you met?"

Betty changed the subject, determined not to get into one of those tight discussions with Abner she never could win. "You keep your scientific approach over in Laboratory Evaluation," she ordered. "Now, then, yes or no, do you come to the celebration barbecue or don't you? Mom's having a ball! She wants to show off her successful daughter to every unmarried fellow in Wyoming."

"Did you say a week from Sunday?"

"I said a week from Sunday."

"I'm busy. I'll buy you a pre-celebration dinner, though. Afterward, we'll drive. When we reach a scenic place I'll propose again, and you'll refuse again, and I'll go home wondering why I bother with you. The pattern as before."

"Is it my fault I'm in love with Luke?"

Abner's hazel eyes chided her. Her cheeks burning, Betty rose and went to the window and looked out at the view. "You know," she told him, keeping her back to him, "it's always a mistake to assume a woman is primarily emotional. I'll concede the obvious fact that a woman is usually more emotional than she ought to be. But we have intellects, too, Mr. Pritchard; we're able to reason in our fashion and arrive at demonstrably valid conclusions. If I say I'm in love with Luke, the statement may seem emotional gaucherie, but it's also a statement of fact."

"Or you would have me believe it to be fact. I often wonder why. Who is this Abner Pritchard? A blend of virtues and vices, a melange of scientific knowledge and some administrative know how and much ignorance. Handsome? I think not. An arresting personality? I know not. A man constrained to run, run, run because so many women find in him the solid character of their dreams? Clearly not. Then why do you work so hard to convince me the fellow is Luke and that I'm wasting valuable time? Other women don't seem to believe excuses or explanations are necessary. In fact, they don't seem to know Abner Pritchard exists."

"It's my mother's fault, I'm afraid. Behold a creature trained to be fair to the weaker sex! Well, you're told and you're warned, Abner. If you're dreadfully disappointed one day, please remember you were told and warned."

He smiled cheerfully, did Abner Pritchard, a compact, rather muscular man of medium stature, his hair a rich and curly chestnut, his eyes hazel, his face quite acceptable if not handsome. "I have been told and warned," he admitted. "Anything else to say? My instincts tell me you didn't ask me to drop in so that you could invite me to a barbecue a week from Sunday."

Reminded, Betty sat down again and looked through her notes. "A small matter, Abner, I've been tracking down a few reports originated by the Laboratory Evaluation Department. I've been told that although they were classified confidential or secret at the time, the projects are obsolete and that it wouldn't matter if the information contained in those reports fell into enemy hands. One report involves the Abernathy missile checkout system."

"Whoa," Abner ordered. And now his manner underwent a great change. He stood up belligerently. "Any man who tells you that information couldn't be used by an enemy is either teasing you or is badly misinformed. Frankly, I hope he's merely teasing you, Betty. I hope we have no one aboard this Center who presumes to think he knows what a potential enemy can or cannot use against us."

"What is this particular checkout system, Abner—in nontechnical language, please?"

"A collection of electronic devices designed to check the HOWLER air-to-air missile before it's loaded onto Navy aircraft. You check the missile primarily to make certain it will function correctly after it's been launched by the pilot."

"But we don't use the HOWLER any more."

"Right. But how do you know, Betty, that every major country in the world has developed a missile as good as the HOWLER? And that's why I say the fellow who told you that nonsense is either teasing you or is badly misinformed. Those reports contain information that would be extremely useful to a power not as advanced in missile technology as we. Hence, the information is still classified confidential or secret. Why should we spend a billion to acquire military information and then give the information to another power?"

Betty nibbled her underlip, beginning to feel quite troubled about Mr. Harold Herman. Although she hated to ask the next question, she did ask it outright, looking straight at the assignment head of the Laboratory Evaluation Department.

"Then you would consider it serious, Abner, if certain of these reports were missing from the reports section of the library?"

He whistled. "So that explains your transfer to Tech Info, eh? I wondered."

"You said that, Abner; not I."

He chuckled. "All right. Question withdrawn. To answer yours, though: I would be disturbed if I knew copies of those reports couldn't be located. I would be so disturbed, in fact, that I would recommend to the Tech Info security agent she conduct an all-out search to learn what happened to the missing reports. You see, Betty, we happen to be working on a missile whose design includes many of the best features of the HOWLER. Need I say more?"

It occurred to Betty after he'd left that the next thing she needed was some expert guidance. She telephoned Fred Teller and made an appointment to eat lunch with him out on the airstrip, where they could discuss the matter without fear of eavesdroppers. Fred came late, and they had to eat in silence for a time because one of the experimental aircraft was being tuned up over near the main hangar. But the turbojet was finally shut off and the mechanics went into the hangar, presumably to eat their own lunches. Fred eyed their departing figures enviously. "I always longed to be a mechanic," he confided. "Just never could get the knack of handling tools, though. What's the problem?"

He listened without interruption while Betty briefed him. Then, his face and voice expressionless, he announced: "Sanderson, you have two problems. The first problem is to locate the missing copies of the reports. The second problem is to make every person in Tech Info so security conscious the carelessness will end."

Fred studied the sky for a time, as if the great cumulus clouds fascinated him. Suddenly a parachute blossomed high over the rolling hills and range.

Betty jumped to her feet, pointing. Fred looked and shrugged. "New type of 'chute. They've been testing it for several weeks. No live tests so far. That's a dummy swinging on the shrouds. They've got that dummy so loaded with devices they can practically measure the velocity of every breeze blowing against it. Now if you'd been smart, if you'd listened to me, you'd be working in Lab Evaluation or Flight Test, and you'd be in the middle of interesting events. But no. You had to have Tech Info. Look, do you think I didn't know things were in a snarl over there? Why do you think I warned you not to demand Tech Info?"

"I didn't demand it. The decision to assign me to Tech Info was made in New York, by Mr. King Abernathy himself."

Fred snapped his gray head back. "Hey," he said hoarsely, "what gives?"

Betty was astonished, for this was her field supervisor talking—and confessing ignorance of the details of her assignment! Stalling for time, she asked: "What's your opinion of George Masters, Fred? It's difficult for me to appraise him because he is the father of my beloved."

"Good printer; no self discipline. Look, maybe this is unnecessary talk, but I'd better remind you I'm technically your boss and that bosses can't help the hired hands if they don't brief him completely. Are you there to tighten up security before the DAGGER III project comes to the Center?"

"Yup." Betty met his eyes briefly and shrugged. "I'm to be very tough, Fred. If I consider it advisable, I'm to fire a couple of Tech Info employees to frighten the others into obeying every regulation on the books."

Betty dug into her handbag, found her instruction sheet and passed it over to Fred. She finished her lunch while he read and reread and thought.

He nodded. "I've been in the same sort of situation myself," he said, and now his voice was briskly professional. "You handle it this way. First you do some more snooping to make sure of all your facts. Then you go to Herman with your stuff. You demand an opportunity to address all the Tech Info employees at a meeting. You lay it on the line. You say that if every missing report isn't returned to the library within a week, you'll turn the department upside down. You also remind them all that being discharged for violation of security regulations can wreck their careers permanently."

"Roll out the cannon, in other words?" Betty frowned, not liking the idea. "I prefer less violent methods."

"But those take time, and how do you know you have time? Suppose New York sent checkers out here to find out how well you're watchdogging Tech Info?"

"So soon?"

"I have news for you, Betty. The DAGGER III research and development project puts this division of the King Abernathy Corporation into the big time. I'm not joking when I say New York will be rough on everyone who jeopardizes that contract."

For the first time, her new assignment frightened Betty Sanderson. She wondered who in the world she was to hold such an important job in such an important department as Tech Info. Perhaps she couldn't handle the job! After all, the exploit that had attracted King Abernathy's attention had really been just a routine arrest made under highly favorable conditions. She'd not had to use her brains unduly to outthink or outmaneuver anyone.

Fred looked at his wristwatch and grunted. "Big

powwow with the chief at once. I'll discuss your problems with him, but I won't imply they're too big for you. I don't really think they are too big for you, Betty. You've been in Security long enough for me to get a pretty good idea of your capabilities. But I'll keep an eye on it all from a distance. If you need help, I'll provide it."

"Nice of you, Fred."

He reached out and gave her brunette head a fatherly pat. "Ah," he said, "what kind of world would it be if folks didn't help out when they could. About Pritchard, incidentally, I had dinner with him the other night. It's now rather definite that he'll take over Lab Evaluation on the first of July. Wykoff is moving up the ladder. He'll be assistant technical director in one of the corporation's plants in New Jersey. Pritchard has been discussing the Jolly S Ranch with the bank people. They'll let him take over the mortgage for an extra two thousand dollars. He thinks you're nuts to want a run-down place like that, but he told me he'd even buy you a hunk of worthless desert if that would make you happy. Fine fellow, Pritchard!"

"Will you stop that?" Betty demanded.

Yet she was deeply moved by the news he loved her that deeply. She wondered how in the world she, of all people, had attracted the attention of two men as fine as Luke and Abner.

6

At forty-four, Mrs. Hazel Sanderson was disinclined to believe that anything less than serious illness or severe pain was a problem of any consequence. When she finally noticed toward the end of June that her daughter was preoccupied and appeared worried, she literally took Betty by the ear and led her outdoors to what she was pleased to call their "rosarium." Mrs. Sanderson said firmly: "Look, and then feel ashamed. You live in the loveliest state of the Union; you have a good job, enjoy good health, are sought by two fine men. You leave the gloom to the antelopes. And they ought to be gloomy, considering the dreadful uses to which man these days is putting what used to be very fine rangeland."

Betty noticed that the talisman climbers were beginning to put on a fine show. She also noticed that beyond the rosarium the rangeland was magnificent under a powder-blue sky. Quite suddenly, she wanted to saddle up and ride. For just one day she wanted to forget all about lost technical reports and hush-hush military secrets and the oddly frightened

Mr. Harold Herman. She wanted to ride to the mountains themselves. She wanted to scale the stony ramparts and inhale air never before inhaled by a human being.

"Any work scheduled?" she asked her mother. "I could use a day out doors."

Her mother colored. "Well, I did invite Mr. O'Neal to lunch. The poor man was telling me it's been years since he's eaten a proper home-cooked meal."

Betty recalled him only vaguely. "Isn't he the man who owns all those trucks?"

"Well, owning trucks isn't really his business, dear. He's really the O'Neal Transportation Company. He does quite well, too. Regardless of what the freight is, he transports it. Mr. Meyer thinks that Mr. Edward O'Neal is a coming power in the economic life of this corner of Wyoming."

Betty's brown eyes danced.

"No such thing!" Mrs. Sanderson denied. "I do hope I'm not so desperate I must marry a man for his money."

"Now *that* thought occurred to you, Mom; not to me. Why would the ugly duckling of the beautiful lady think she had to marry for loot?"

"The fact is," Hazel Sanderson went on, "that money means little to me. All I really want is to own this ranch again. Is that a silly aspiration, do you think? I often wonder. But it meant so much to your father and me. Betty, I know you won't believe this, but your father and I did most of the building out here. We started with a shack, and we huffed and we puffed and we managed to build yonder house."

Betty almost said wearily that she'd heard the story before. But then it occurred to her that these memories were important to her mother, that through them she found the justification for life that everyone had to find sooner or later.

"Tell more," she said. "It makes me proud, really it does, to know I'm the daughter of real pioneers."

"Little to tell, when you come down to it. We built and we prospered, and you came, and everything seemed perfect. Then John died, and things were less perfect."

Her mother shot Betty a sharp glance.

"Do you mourn your dead forever," she asked, "or do you close the door at last and remarry? What are your views on the subject of my remarriage?"

"I'll give the bride away, happily and proudly."

Her mother laughed so relievedly that Betty wondered if Mr. Edward O'Neal was destined to become her second father.

She decided that she didn't want to go riding after all. "What would Ed love for lunch?" she asked. "Good old Ed with all those trucks and such!"

"*I'll* prepare the lunch, thank you."

Mrs. Sanderson nipped back to the house, very pink now, as much atwitter about the lunch guest as any girl about her first date. All things considered, it was just as well that she did practically barricade herself into the kitchen, for about ten minutes later an attractive black-haired woman came riding at a canter up the earthen road between the trees. The woman proved to be Mrs. Calvin Abernathy of the Wobbly W. "Hi," she said easily, dismounting. "I thought it about time I paid you folks a visit. I understand our cattle displease you."

Betty took her hand and led her into the patio. "Technically," she admitted, "it's the bank's business, not ours, if your cattle trespass. I just mentioned it to Mr. Abernathy in passing, ma'am."

"Ma'am? At my tender age? Betty Sanderson, don't make me cross. I'm Alicia. And for your information, I used to be a slave of the monster at the test center. I was the first female technical editor they ever hired, in fact."

Her deep blue eyes said more, so much more that Betty began to understand there was more to this visit than was obvious.

"Coffee? Lemonade? I'd invite you to lunch, Alicia, but it seems that my mother is to have a special guest."

"Nothing, thanks. Nice place you have here. I've often thought about making a business deal with you folks. Let me tell you something. When I bought the Wobbly W with my very own money I was more or less in your position. Lots of land, good buildings, no stock, and good grass going to waste. A rancher arranged with me to use my land in exchange for range upkeep and so many calves a year. I had the nucleus of a good herd when I married."

"Really?"

"And I was a city girl, Betty; not a ranch girl, like you. These things can be done if a person is clever and lucky. In my case, of course, it was all luck. The rancher came to me with the idea, you see."

Betty dropped onto the chaise longue and smiled politely and waited for Mrs. Calvin Abernathy to make her point. There was a point, Betty was positive. Although this was the first time she had met the former Alice Clarke, she had a good working knowledge of the woman's intelligence and resourcefulness. New York born and bred and educated, the daughter of author Agnes Clarke and a talented writer herself, Miss Alice Clarke was already something of a legend in the Wyoming division of the King Abernathy Corporation. Not only had she demonstrated that a woman could hold her own in a highly technical field, but she had also demonstrated that a woman could transform an exuberant, fun-loving executive into a general manager worth his salt almost before he knew what had happened. Such a woman, Betty was sure, would hardly ride out to the Jolly S at this late date merely to make her acquaintance or give her an opportunity to achieve her ambition to get the Jolly S out of the bank's clutches.

Alice Abernathy seemed to sense the reason for her silence. The woman grinned. "Try again, eh? A reasonable attitude, considering that we've been neighbors for six years and haven't met before. Very well. I'm somewhat concerned about my husband, Miss Sanderson. He's behaved most oddly of late. Finally, I managed to worm some of his worries out of him. You seem to be the particular worry."

"I?"

"Miss Sanderson, allow me to give you some information you may lack. The *New York Recorder* is a conservative and highly responsible newspaper. It's unthinkable that they should endeavor to obtain unauthorized photographs of the first flight test of the DAGGER II missile. I'm convinced that the cameras of those men you arrested were not loaded with film. I'm also convinced that their attempt to penetrate into the Surface-Launch area was made with the full knowledge of my husband's uncle in New York. Had he not known in advance of the attempt, Mr. King Abernathy would have publicized the matter for all he was worth to prove to the world the unwisdom of trying to sneak in under one of his fences. Reasonable deduction so far?"

"You're talking and I'm listening, Mrs. Abernathy."

Mrs. Abernathy smiled and continued.

"Proof that Uncle King knew what was going on can be found in the records of your department,

Miss Sanderson. The order to fly the reporters to New York, the order for Chief Hoyt to accompany them to New York, the order to squash what could have been a sensational newspaper story. And you. My dear Miss Sanderson, the best that can be said of your accomplishment that day is that you did your job, the job you are paid to do. Yet for this you receive the order of merit, a handsome promotion, a position of responsibility and an assignment made by Uncle King himself. Doesn't all this seem as odd to you as to me?"

"Mine not to reason why, Mrs. Abernathy. That's particularly true when you're engaged in security work. At the time you're hired you're told you must be prepared to give your life if need be to safeguard our defense secrets. And you're also told that orders are to be obeyed, not questioned. I imagine Chief Hoyt convinced Mr. Abernathy I'm qualified to watchdog Tech Info. I imagine your success in the corporation inclined Mr. Abernathy to give me an opportunity to get ahead."

Mrs. Calvin Abernathy asked embarrassingly: "Or is my husband a flop, Miss Sanderson?"

Betty pitied her then, realizing it must have cost her a great deal to ask the question. For about a minute or so she proceeded to forget she was a security agent. "No such thing!" she said vehemently. "Your husband is actually the most respected man at the Center, and I'm not polishing any apples, either. Now look. Naturally I can't divulge my assignment to you. But I certainly can say that nothing I'm involved in can possibly embarrass Mr. Abernathy in any way."

The silence was long. During the silence, Mrs. Abernathy's mount grew restless and wandered off to to browse on Jolly S grass. For once, Betty didn't object to the greed of Wobbly W stock. She loved the sight the powerful chestnut gelding made as it headed for a particularly succulent-looking stand of grass. Her own Danny, she thought, didn't compare with the gelding at all favorably.

Mrs. Abernathy nodded. When she smiled, it was a true smile, a smile with genuine warmth in it, the smile of one woman to another woman. "Glad to hear it," Mrs. Abernathy said. "A wife worries. You know how it is."

She'd barely gone when a white Cadillac convertible came whizzing in from the highway. The big, brawny, twinkling-eyed Irisher who got out had to be none other than Mr. Edward O'Neal, so Betty gave him the warmest greeting she could without tipping her mother's hand. "Wonderful surprise, sir," she said. "Mom is inside preparing something fancy. Care to watch her or look over the ranch?"

"What ranch, lass?"

"Now do I belittle your trucks, Mr. O'Neal? Such as the ranch is, it's a ranch."

"Needs stock. Needs cleaning up a bit, and then some more. Now don't flash your sassy brown eyes like that! O'Neal is a man of peace. If he calls a spade a spade, it's only to clear the air, so to speak. How old are you?"

"Almost twenty-four."

"Why aren't you married? O'Neal will have to fix that, I'm thinking. Girl, let's have an understanding here and now. Not in seven hundred years has an O'Neal woman died a spinster! Another thing. Pants are for men to wear, not girls. And what do you think of that?"

Betty did think that this handsome Irisher with the graying temples was much more nervous, and therefore belligerent, than he ought to be. "I think," she said placatingly, "that I'll love having you as a father, sir, if and when you learn not to yell. Such noise! You deafen me!"

Their eyes met.

His ruddy face softened. "Ah, lass," he said, "the O'Neal women have always had discerning eyes and understanding hearts. And will you give the bride away, do you think?"

Betty was startled. "Then it's decided?"

"If it wasn't," he roared, "would I be here fancied up while there's money to be made in trucking?"

He gave Betty's cheek a smacking kiss and her bottom a stinging wallop. "Tell Hazel to hurry," he ordered. "A man could starve to death here on this bonny blue Sabbath morning."

7

George Masters said woozily: "I'm happy for your mother, Betty. Your mother is a fine woman. Your mother took it on the chin like a man. Never a wimper. After your father died, she hocked the ranch and got a job and put you through college. Women like your mother are the people who make this country great. I'm glad she's getting something for herself after all these years."

He reached for the bourbon. He filled his glass and raised it high. "To Hazel," he toasted. "May she always be happy."

He downed the drink, heaved a sentimental sigh and settled back in the wicker porch chair. Before them, the range was purple in the oncoming dusk. Already the hills had lost their details, and even the range was becoming a blur of undistinguishable vegetation. Soon, Betty thought, the antelope would be out and the coyotes would be prowling.

"You'll like O'Neal," George prophesied confidently. "Everybody likes O'Neal. You want to know why you'll like O'Neal? I'll tell you. O'Neal would rather hand you a dollar than break your nose. If every rich, self-made man had the heart of O'Neal, the Communists wouldn't stand a chance here."

"Do you think they do stand a chance here? Pop, it seems to me you've celebrated my mother's good news quite long enough. How did the Communists become involved in her engagement?"

"Why do you always call me Pop? I'm not your Pop. Let me tell you something. Being somebody's Pop is a very serious business. And what does it get you? The mother dies in childbirth; you have to raise the boy. And does the boy want to be a printer? The trade isn't good enough for him. The printing press has done more for man than any invention since the wheel, but learning to set type and run the press isn't good enough for the boy."

Betty reached surreptitiously for the bottle of bourbon. He noticed, slapped, but she whisked the bottle out of his reach anyway. He said grumpily: "If there are two things I can't stand, they're a snoop and a bluenose. Go on home, Sanderson. Let's make more missiles with nuclear warheads to kill more people in a minute than cancer does in a century. Fine work we're all doing, isn't it?"

Betty did want to leave then. Suddenly she wanted to leave more than she wanted to do anything else in years. She disliked the savagery deep in George Masters' eyes. She disliked the wagging, critical tongue. She hated sitting there, listening to his whiskey-befuddled talk. Still, she decided grimly, it was her job to listen.

"What's really wrong with our work?" she asked conversationally. "As I see it all, Pop, we're involved in an arms race with the Communist world. If we don't do this work, what happens? Seriously, do you really think a lot of countries in this world wouldn't love to see our country reduced to impotency?"

"Somebody has to set a good example."

"Well, we've offered to disarm, you know. All President Kennedy and President Johnson have asked is that an inspection system be established to make sure no one cheats."

"Don't I read the newspapers? I can even print newspapers. But somebody has to set a good example, as I said. Why not us? What are we afraid of?"

"We're afraid of having our teeth kicked out once we've lost our power to defend ourselves, Pop."

"Maybe Luke is right, at that," he said. "At least a doctor thinks life is sacred. You and me, Sanderson, you know what we are? Agents of death."

A horse and rider came across the purpling land; not a dude engineer or a scientist playing at being a cowboy, but a fellow who sat his mount well and rode as if riding were his business. He came onto the property by way of the brook trail, and about five hundred yards from the frame house he halted to let his horse drink. An interesting thing happened. He waved at George Masters, and the squat printer waved back. Then without apology or explanation, George Masters struggled to his feet and went over to the brook to powwow with the rider. For a time the two men seemed to be on friendly terms. But an argument began and the first thing Betty knew, George was trying to punch the rider. She was up and running as quickly as possible, but long before she could intervene George was sitting on the ground, complaining bitterly about dirty fighters who shoved rather than punched. The rider, a lean, hawkeyed man in his late twenties, gave Betty a bewildered look. "Lady girl," he drawled, "what's wrong with this buzzard? He tells me to come to do some work, so

I come. He's real friendly, then he ain't? You ask me, him and John Barleycorn ain't the good friends that this fellow thinks they are."

With the fellow's help, Betty got George back to a chair on the porch. George fussed and fumed for a time, then told Betty he felt some cussing coming on and that she'd better leave before she was shocked. Betty ambled back to the brook with the rider, and she sat down under one of the trees and studied first him and then his mount. "Long way from the Wobbly W," she commented. "It must have been a fine ride."

"Duke Elliot, lady girl. Peeler. They've sure got some broncs to peel there, too. Understand their last peeler is still in the hospital."

"Sage King. Have you tried Sage King yet, Mr. Elliott? I visited Clay Singleton the other evening, and he tells me Sage King has a nasty reverse weave you have to watch out for. He tears to the right, then shifts violently to the left like greased lightning. That was the trick that unseated Clay."

"I do things a little different, lady girl. I run them ragged first—the tough ones, I mean. By the time I hit the saddle, there ain't too much fight left in them. I've got a heap of admiration for Clay, don't ever think otherwise. But to Clay, it was always a sort of duel between him and the bronc, a duel they scrapped out on real fair terms. Kid stuff, to me. You hire out to peel a bronc, not to fight no duel. You don't kill the horse, you don't hurt the horse, but you sure don't give him any breaks."

"Sensible," Betty conceded.

Duke gaze toward the porch. "Sure hope the old gaffer ain't sore at me," he said worriedly. "I can use the *dinero* he promised. These days around Antelope View, it's hard to earn *dinero* unless you're one of them missile engineers or scientists. Just a few ranches left, and their bunkhouses are full up."

"Oh, Pop will simmer down. He has one of these private drinking bouts about once a month. He gets all his frustrations out of him, and then he's the nicest fellow you could meet."

"Pop? Hey, I didn't know he had a daughter!"

"I just call him that," Betty explained. "What sort of work were you going to do for him? Pop has no broncs to peel that I know of."

"Dude cowboy stuff. He knows some fellows who want to spend a week or so moseying around the rangeland. I sort of shepherd them around, make sure they don't get lost or starve."

An idea occurred to Betty. "Suppose I were to tell you, Duke, that the bank and I own the Jolly S ranch and that I'd like to run some stock. Then suppose I were to tell you I have little money, no stock and no hired hands. Could you start with just found and maybe fifty a month if you were promised a better deal as things improved?"

His blue eyes narrowed. He sat watching the brook as the evening purple deepened all around them. "A fellow would have to hear more," he finally said. "What I mean is, would you try to build up to a real ranch, would I have a chance to be foreman, would I maybe get a share of the profits some day? I don't hone to do a lot of work for nothing."

"I'll build it up, Duke. Let me be frank with you. My mother's interest in the ranch was turned over to me last week. Mr. O'Neal, who's engaged to marry my mother, has promised me a certain sum of money with which to buy stock and fix things up. You know Edward O'Neal?"

"Who don't? That fellow could pick up a rock and make with the Irish blarney and turn that rock into gold. So it's your mother he's marrying, huh? Well, that makes things different. I guess I could be hired for found and fifty and a chance. I'm getting worried, boss lady. The way the ranches are closing down around in these parts, a fellow could darned well go through life without never being foreman of a real spread."

They shook hands on it just as Luke came driving in from one of his emergency calls. Betty got into Luke's car for the brief ride back to the house and Luke, of course, was all curiosity about the handsome cowboy. "A rival?" he asked. "I'll challenge him to a draw."

"Foreman of the Jolly S ranch—eventually," Betty told him casually. "I can't help being a brilliant businesswoman. Look who my mother is!"

"Okay," Dr. Luke Masters admitted, "that was sheer jealousy talking. Question withdrawn. What about waiting here until I get Pop into bed? I'll saddle some horses, and we'll ride."

"Where to?"

"To anywhere. What about to the area where you arrested those reporters? I'd like to see the place where you won your order of merit."

Betty managed to say calmly that the idea sounded good to her. But after the men had gone indoors she felt so frightened suddenly she wanted to race back home in her car. Great day in the morning, she wondered, *how had Luke known about those reporters?* There'd been no publicity!

8

FRED TELLER denied heatedly that there could have been a leak. "The boys don't leak information to anyone," Fred snapped, "and I resent the insinuation they leaked info concerning those reporters."

"Dr. Luke Masters knew about it, Fred. Also, he knew the section in which the reporters were arrested."

"Maybe *you* gave the show away? Take a moonlit night with romance in the air. Maybe you were so carried away you dropped enough info he could put two and two together?"

"Nope."

"And I say the boys didn't leak info, so where are we?"

Chief Hoyt intervened, speaking a bit loudly because of the drumming rain. "Let's cut out the argument," Chief Hoyt suggested. "I don't think the boys talked, I don't think Sanderson talked. That leaves two other possibilities. Either the reporters were bigger loud-mouths than we thought, or Ma Hooper did some bragging in her greasy spoon."

"Not Ma Hooper," Betty said confidently. "She was never told that the reporters did come along and were arrested. In fact, I was very careful to let her believe the fellows were just talkative tourists."

"The reporters didn't talk about the arrest, either," Fred said thoughtfully. "Wouldn't make sense for them to brag about failure."

"So?" Chief Hoyt asked.

The final possibility alarmed Betty. She said tautly: "Luke must have gotten the information from his father. I know that. But from whom did his father get it?"

It was Fred Teller, typically, who finally asked the question in all their minds. "Do you think Masters helped those reporters, folks? Let's analyze the situation. Two strangers come here from New York. They're here just two days. On the second day they hit our fence less than two hundred yards from a little hill that commands a view of the Surface-Launch area. Accidental? My eye! Also, they approached the right spot by crossing some of the least desirable and least used rangeland in the Antelope View vicinity. Accidental? Again, my eye! Those fellows knew exactly where they were going and the best way to get there undetected. They couldn't have picked up all that information in just a day of scouting around. So that means they had a contact inside this Center. Well, do you think Masters helped them? Masters worked as a printer in New York. Printers know reporters, and vice versa. Logical, Illogical? What?"

"Possible," Chief Hoyt agreed. He shot Betty a troubled glance. "Now this may surprise you," he said, "but the idea of an inside contact occurred to me, too. In New York, when we questioned the reporters, we put that query to them. They refused to answer on the grounds that reporters must protect their sources of information. Mr. King Abernathy never could make them admit they had an inside contact, but we all had the feeling they did."

"What would Mr. Masters gain from helping them, sir?" Betty asked.

"Who knows, Sanderson? Maybe Masters wants to work in New York again. George Masters is a mixed-up character. Does a great job here in one way, but a lousy job in other ways. And let's face it. Respect for security regulations just isn't in George Masters."

Fred Teller looked at Betty, regret on his face but not in his tone. "You know what to do?" he asked.

Betty said glumly that she knew what to do.

Fred understood the glumness. "Yeah," he said, "real tough. If I were in your shoes, I wouldn't be cheering, either. You can always ask for a transfer, you know."

Chief Hoyt said sharply: "Nope."

Fred looked at the chief. "Sir," he queried, "how come? It isn't as if Sanderson here is the only one we can assign to this job. I'm free enough to handle it myself, in fact."

"Very simple," Chief Hoyt said. "Is Sanderson a security agent or isn't she? She takes seven thousand a year for being a security agent. Okay. So if I can ask an agent to risk his neck, I can ask an agent to risk some temporary embarrassment."

But there was more here than met the eye. After she had thought about it for ten or fifteen seconds, Betty decided that what was involved was nothing less than the natural curiosity of a boss to determine if one of his workers had it in her to subordinate friendship to the requirements of her work. Appreciating his position, Betty asked the almost inevitable question: "What happens if I goof, sir?"

"It's the trying that counts, Sanderson. I don't like

mistakes or failures, of course. Who does? But if you honestly try, I won't complain."

Betty nodded and shrugged. "I won't like doing it, naturally," she said. "Still, I accepted the work, sir, didn't I?"

Fred, his expression grim, led her back along the hall to his office. He closed the door and waved Betty to a chair. He studied her troubled face a moment with the manner of a fellow who wondered why anyone in his right mind undertook to do security work. Once he had sat down, however, Fred was a tough turkey and all business.

"As I've gotten the full story from the chief," he said, "you were assigned to Tech Info to tighten up security there, no matter what. And you were also instructed to find a patsy and fire him if that was the best way to make everyone in Tech Info security conscious. Okay. Your patsy is George Masters. So the first thing you do is rowel him. You barge into the print shop and find something to squawk about, and you squawk. Tomorrow you do the same thing, and you keep needling him until he gets sore. To discipline him, you recommend his suspension. No matter what Herman says, you hold out for suspension. Then at the strategic time, you demand his head. Masters' head, that is. Understood?"

"Suppose we're wrong, Fred?"

"Won't make any difference. We need a patsy or a sacrificial lamb to make the others handle classified information with care. George Masters is the logical guy to use. He drinks too much. He doesn't approve of our work. Worse, he talks too much."

"And what do I do about Luke?"

"I like Luke. I think he's a very fine character. I think he ought to be given a medal for trying to establish a practice here instead of in a big city where he could probably earn a fortune. But for my dough, the real fellow for you is Pritchard. Therefore, I won't weep if Luke gets sore at you and crosses you off his list."

"But I may weep, and what then?"

"I hear tell your mother is marrying O'Neal, baby. I also hear tell the Jolly S Ranch may make a real big comeback. You don't have to work here. You can resign here and now if you like, and there'll be no black mark in your record. So why don't you think everything over? The chief wants action today, but I can stall him."

"You would stall him?" Betty asked.

Fred was pained. "Look," he said, "I may be the chief's tough assistant and your immediate boss, but I'm also a guy who has a heart. Why do you think I questioned the chief when he said you couldn't transfer?"

"You're nice," Betty told him. "It's a privilege to work under you, Fred."

His hatchet face grew red, and he turned testy. "Don't butter me up, Sanderson," he barked. "I'd do as much for a dog."

He gestured, and that was it. Betty had to jeep back to the Technical Information Building to get the unpleasantness begun. She spent an hour familiarizing herself with the record George Masters had made since the day twelve years before when he had begun work at the Center as an offset press operator. Then, feeling cold and wretched, she walked the long walk to the print shop to give Mr. George Masters a bad time.

He greeted her grumpily as she entered his small, windowless office. "Scat," he ordered. "We have a high-priority report to get out for Dr. Schroeder. It has to be on a midnight plane."

"Business, business, business, George. I'm still trying to locate that report on the reliability of the Abernathy missile checkout system. Secret documents just can't disappear in my department."

"Drop dead."

Betty put iron into her voice. "No, George. Security comes first, then that report of Dr. Schroeder. Let's take everyone off the job and find the missing report, shall we?"

He was speechless.

While he was speechless, Betty went out into the big print shop and blew her police whistle. She announced with forced cheerfulness that they would find the missing reliability report if they had to hang around all that night. George at once roared for everyone to get back to work. His eyes blazing, he then told Betty to get out of his print shop or he'd throw her out.

At that point, Irene Crawford, George's assistant, tried to intervene. "Mr. Masters," she protested, "you just can't argue with Security that way. And when it's a question of listening to you or Miss Sanderson, we have to listen to Miss Sanderson."

"You're fired!" George yelled. "Anybody not on the job in ten seconds is fired!"

Some started to go back to work, but Irene stopped them. Irene did more. She rushed into George's office and telephoned Mr. Herman, and presently the dapper Mr. Herman came hurrying in, all concern.

George yelled at Mr. Herman that he was being paid to print reports, not to look for needles in a haystack. Mr. Herman automatically asked Betty if the report couldn't be printed first. "After all," Mr. Herman said most reasonably, "a report by our chief scientist, Miss Sanderson, is a matter of some importance, too."

Betty asked frigidly if she had his permission to telephone Chief Hoyt. Mr. Herman blanched. He turned to George Masters and said: "We'll have to live with this, sir. I'll inform Dr. Schroeder of the reason for the delay. Naturally, we must humor Security now."

Mr. George Masters finally gave the order for the search to begin, but it seemed to Betty that now was as good a time as any for her to wax tough. "Don't you search, sir," she told George. "Mr. Herman, will you suspend Mr. Masters for a week, please, for impeding a security agent in the performance of her work?"

9

The requested suspension was processed first by the Technical Information Department, then by the Industrial Relations Office, and finally by Calvin Abernathy's administrative assistant, Arnold Pagano. Each officer recommended that the suspension be canceled because of extenuating circumstances. Under other conditions, Calvin Abernathy would have honored the recommendations and chewed out the Security Department for making a mountain out of a molehill. But when he discussed the matter with his wife, Alice said sharply: "Slow down, buckaroo. Really, Cal, you're the most impetuous general manager I've ever met. What's the full story? Do you even know the full story?"

He laughed and ruffled her glossy hair. On this late-July evening they were eating dinner in the patio of the adobe ranchhouse, all the world beautiful before them, particularly the flame and gold sky. "More steak," he ordered. "I may become the fattest general manager you've ever met."

"Fetch it yourself," she said smugly. "Pregnant women are supposed to be coddled."

He fetched it himself from the barbecue grille. After he'd eaten awhile, he returned to the suspension matter. "The full story is quickly told," he said. "The agent made a reasonable request, and George Masters was unreasonable. On the other hand, George was under pressure to get a hot report ready for a midnight plane to Washington. Moreover, George can always be depended upon to get hot reports out to meet even tough deadlines. Moreover, George has been with us twelve years and has climbed the ladder on the basis of ability. All these things considered, I think the security agent should have handled the matter differently."

"Do you know her?"

"Not too well. She has a good record and certainly has courage. I'm not so sure she has good judgment, however."

"I've met her, and I disagree. I thought she is a discerning young lady who knows when to speak and when to listen."

"How come you met her?"

"Some indirect complaints about our cattle reached my ears," Alice fibbed easily. "I thought a discussion was in order, so I rode over to the Jolly S."

"In your condition?"

"I didn't know about my condition at the time. Incidentally, you must not think of pregnancy as a condition of illness. Ask my mother. My mother has written a definitive book on the subject. In the book she actually argues that non-pregnancy is the condition to fret about. Anyway, I found Miss Betty Sanderson to be an interesting, well-controlled, quite intelligent young woman."

Lanky Calvin Abernathy pondered this, relating it

to his own appraisal of the girl who had one morning arrested two newspaper reporters and had won the order of merit in the process.

"She needled George Masters pretty effectively," he went on. "Even Herman heard some of that. It almost seemed, according to Herman, that she was determined to provoke Masters into some stupid act."

"Ah!"

Calvin blinked.

Without a word, Alice Abernathy went into the house. She came back about five minutes later with a letter. "From your beloved uncle, the great tycoon," she said. "Now hear this. I quote. Security must be tightened out there, Alice. We'll use any method we can, even if it appears cruel, to establish the requisite environment for the development of the DAGGER III missile. In the long history of our corporation, we have never before been engaged in a project so essential to the safety of our country. I tell you all this so that you will curb Cal's hot temper whenever and however one of his precious employees appears to be given a raw deal by our Security Department. Unquote, husband."

Cal winced, beginning to understand. "And the first palsy is George Masters?"

"So it would seem."

"I hate it," Cal said passionately. "Do you hear? I hate it! Masters may be grouchy and rude, but he's a good worker and a loyal American."

"How do you know about the latter, Cal? I hate to sound like a technical editor, but you make so many statements based upon opinion rather than fact. Specifically, how do you know the Security Department hasn't discovered he's a serious security risk?"

"They would have to say so, and in writing."

"Only if they wanted him fired. But if they just wanted to teach him a lesson?"

Cal Abernathy growled and went into the house. He found the telephone number of Miss Betty Sanderson and peremptorily ordered her to come discuss her suspension request at his home. The speed with which she came in her Ford sedan rather disturbed him. Whether she was right or wrong in the matter, she certainly appeared to have the courage of her convictions. Taking her measure, he decided she could be a rugged brunette when she wished to be. Having decided this, he gave her a charming smile and waved her to a chair beside his wife's.

"Quite informal discussion," he said. "You may speak freely before Alice, Miss Sanderson. She occasionally does work for us and still has government clearance to deal with top secret material."

"Yes, sir."

"I said informal," he reminded her. "I'm Cal; this is Alice. After we've cleared the air a bit, I'll show you around the place. If you wish to remain overnight, fine. I'm supposed to sell you some blooded stock, according to O'Neal. You may look the herd over in the morning."

She smiled, but said neither yes nor no, he noticed.

"Is this Masters question, Miss Sanderson, involved with the secret assignment my uncle gave you?"

"Yes, sir. And it's really no secret any longer, Mr. Abernathy. Security in Tech Info is in a mess. No proof of disloyalty, but certainly every indication of considerable carelessness in the handling of classified material. Further, there is some thought that those newspaper reporters I picked up one morning had an inside contact, and there is slight evidence that Mr. George Masters may be that contact."

Cal noticed that his wife's face went stony. Cal said:

"Strong stuff, all that, Miss Sanderson. Why don't you people ask for Masters' discharge?"

"We will, sir. The question isn't that. The timing is considered most important. We want to extract every benefit we can from the discharge."

"Benefit to whom?"

"To the corporation, of course. It's believed that if the matter is handled correctly, the security snarl in Tech Info will end once and for all."

"And what do you people imagine the Professional Employees' Council will do about all this? Masters is liked and respected. They'll fight for him."

"Yes, sir."

"Why, this could lead to labor trouble! Do you people realize that?"

"Yes, sir."

Just as Cal was about to lose his temper, his wife asked wonderingly: "But aren't you engaged to Dr. Luke Masters, Betty?"

"Informally, Mrs. Abernathy, yes."

Cal swallowed. He said huskily: "Rough assignment, Miss Sanderson. I'm sorry."

"Chief Hoyt tells me that's why I earn seven thousand a year, sir. Of course the salary is quite unimportant. Duty, and all that."

He pursed his lips and frowned. "Well, give me the rest of it, please. Why did my uncle select you, Miss Sanderson? You're junior, very junior, in that department. I should have thought Fred Teller would have been given the assignment."

"Unfortunately, I arrested some clever reporters, sir. Apparently your uncle believed I could handle this matter."

"Can you?"

She did something he admired her for. Although this was an opportunity for her to brag to a wheel, she smiled and reported: "I doubt it, sir. I'll give it a good try, however."

"And did it ever occur to you," Alice Abernathy asked indignantly, "that you may have been selected because you're expendable, Betty Sanderson?"

The shocking question didn't ruffle the calm of the lovely brunette, however. She smiled amiably at Alice and admitted: "Well, that thought has flitted through my mind more than once, Mrs. Abernathy. Still, orders are orders, as Chief Hoyt constantly reminds us."

"Well, I think a certain Abernathy in New York ought to feel ashamed, Betty, and I intend to tell him so."

Alice did, too, that same night, not a half-hour after Betty Sanderson had agreed to spend the night on the Wobbly W. Alice telephoned New York and hung on grimly and battled past servant after servant until she finally got the ear of King Abernathy himself. Alice then proceeded to lay it on the line in a manner that made Calvin proud of her.

"Uncle King," Alice began it, "I'm to be a mother. I'm not bragging, you understand, because other women have been mothers, too. I'm simply telling you this so you'll understand I'm to be accorded civility and patience this night. Is that understood?"

Obviously, it was.

"Very well," Alice said. "Now hear this, Uncle King. I've been through your corporation mill and I'm well aware that sometimes an individual must be sacrificed for the greater good. But why Betty Sanderson?"

Denials.

Alice laughed.

More denials.

Alice said: "Uncle King, you happen to be talking to

an intelligent woman. You'll have to do better than that."

Finally, candor . . . candor that drove the color from Alice's cheeks.

At the end she said weakly: "Thanks, Uncle King. Thank goodness I don't work for you any more."

She sat down after she'd pronged the handset, and she said: "This can be a dirty business, Cal. Did you know that?"

He sighed and nodded.

"The brilliant and courageous security agent, Cal, is a pawn. She knows too little and, paradoxically, too much. The reporters came without Uncle King's knowledge. They asked him what would have happened had they been trained enemy agents? He had to admit she couldn't have shot both before one killed her. So it was a loss and a victory for each side. The newspaper keeps quiet; Uncle King keeps quiet. But just suppose a certain security agent talked?"

10

Luke telephoned several times during his father's week of suspension. Betty refused to talk to him. Knowing her routine rather well, Luke waylaid her on Thursday evening in town as Betty was ambling by City Hall, en route to the public library. Betty grinned and waved amiably, but cold bloodedly beat him to the punch. "I won't discuss your father," she announced. "It's a security matter, period."

"Why are you doing this?" Luke asked hoarsely. "You know what it means, what it must mean."

There was no doubt that Luke had been deeply hurt. His pallid face looked pinched, and there were dark semicircles under his eyes.

"Nice evening," Betty commented, gazing around with studied nonchalance. "I do think, though, that our city fathers ought to hire a gardener and transform that scraggly lawn before the Hall into a garden spot. This isn't a sleepy cattle town of the Old West any more. We ought to fancy up."

Luke gripped her arm. His stubby fingers hurt, but pride prevented Betty from crying out. She met his gray eyes foursquare and said bluntly: "Luke, it would cost me my job to discuss the matter with you. Surely a doctor can understand there are times when one must hold her tongue?"

Without a word, Luke whirled and went across the road to his car. He drove off without regard for the red traffic light. A car barely missed colliding with his, but it was doubtful if Luke even noticed. Shaken by the near accident, Betty turned and hurried on to the library.

At that hour, Miss Dill was alone in the library, and of course bored. She gave Betty a warm hello and asked her please to relate some gossip. Betty told her to be her age, and Miss Dill laughed. "That's my trouble," she confided. "At my age a woman needs loads of gossip if she's to enjoy even vicarious thrills. How is Hazel bearing up under the strain of her engagement?"

"Well, it's difficult, Miss Dill. First of all, this Irisher she's marrying is a man of definite opinions. He thinks they ought to live here in his house in town and make a big splash. Mom, on the other hand, would love to ride herd on me at the Jolly S. Poor Mom is fighting a losing battle, however. First of all, she's nuts about the Irisher. Secondly, he does have excellent business reasons for living in town. Care to room and board with me?"

"Ugh! I'm one woman of the Wild West who does *not* appreciate the wide open spaces and smelly cattle. Do you know Pru Marshall?"

Betty thought, and finally placed the girl. "A new nurse to hit these parts, isn't she? I think I met her at the Women's Club tea."

"She'd probably leap at the chance to live on a ranch. Nice young woman, incidentally. Luke tells me that several patients and one doctor at the hospital have already lost their hearts to her."

Now Betty did sit down, faintly disturbed because Miss Dill had stressed Luke's name. "Ma'am," she asked outright, "does Luke happen to be that doctor?"

Miss Dill switched on a couple of lights. Although her desk was painfully neat, she proceeded to rearrange her rubber stamps and the ink pad and the desk calendar and the box of paper clips. When all was rearranged, Miss Dill said softly: "It's all rather unfortunate, dear. Naturally, most people in town know the circumstances of Mr. Masters' suspension. And don't scowl, please, because not even the great FBI itself can change human nature. People will talk about things of that sort regardless of the consequences. And people will choose sides, of course, and there will always be some who will extend warm-hearted sympathy to the innocent bystander who is also hurt. Am I being clear?"

"You're being clear."

"You must remember, dear, that this can hurt Luke deeply. Through choice, he returned to his home town to establish a practise. The progress has been painfully slow, but there has been progress. Now, just as he's beginning to achieve stature, his father is suspended under circumstances that raise the question of his loyalty to his country."

"No such thing!"

"I'm presenting the matter as others see it, dear. It's the opinion of these others that will make it more difficult than ever for Luke to establish a sound and paying practice. All that considered, isn't it reasonable that the warm-hearted sympathy of an attractive young woman would be most welcome to Luke?"

"A job is a job," Betty said doggedly. "If it's a matter of life and death, a doctor will make his decision and do his best regardless of the consequences. So it must be in missile and space work, Miss Dill—particularly if either is related to national defense. When you think orbital flight is reasonably feasible, you send a Glenn or a Carpenter up. Their lives are on the line. But you send them up and they go up anyway, because that's how things must be. Or you suspend a man because that's how things must be."

"Why not resign?" Miss Dill asked. "As I understand it from Hazel, Mr. O'Neal is giving you the Jolly S free and clear because you welcomed him so warmly into the family. You've always wanted to redevelop the ranch, and now you can. Why continue with a job you won't need and which might be less beneficial than you hope?"

"You don't resign in the middle of a tricky situation, Miss Dill. At least I don't."

The door swung open and a couple of fellows walked in. One was Joel Brower, the head of Tech Info's scientific illustration branch. He hesitated when he saw Betty at the desk, murmured something to his companion, and then limped over and asked diffidently if he could chat with Betty unofficially for a few moments. Betty was exasperated, but gave grudging assent and went outdoors with him to one of the nearby benches.

Joel said without preamble: "You're in a fight, Miss Sanderson. The Professional Employees' Council held a special meeting this afternoon to hear a presentation by George Masters. We finally voted unanimously to back him to the limit. Since I'm the representative for Tech Info, I've been asked to have a talk with you."

"Fair enough, Joel. What do we talk about?"

"Well, Miss Sanderson, it seemed to everyone on the Council that you were unusually rough on George. Say for the sake of argument that he was pretty rude and uncooperative. The normal thing to do is chew the guy out and give him a warning. But you promptly hit him with the loss of a week's wages plus a pretty black mark in his record."

"I didn't know," Betty said carefully, "that a judgment decision could be questioned."

His blue eyes met hers briefly. "We don't question the judgment; just the severity of the penalty. And the higher-ups question that, too. Herman has written a memo of protest; so has Quigley; so has Pagano. So you see, Miss Sanderson, this isn't a case of employees banding together to protect their own. Even upper-bracket administrators are against you."

"Then why don't they cancel the suspension, Joel?"

A muscle quivered in his left cheek. "You know why," he charged bitterly. "Under Chief Hoyt, the Security Department has managed to become a law unto itself. Whenever a matter remotely involves security, the little shots and the big shots run scared."

"But not the Professional Employees' Council?"

"Oh, some of us are scared, all right. But it seems to us, Miss Sanderson, that we have an unhealthy situation here. The workers are supposed to have rights; among them, reasonable assurance that their jobs are theirs to keep so long as they do their work. But as things stand now, any worker can be discharged with impunity at any time if something involving security is raised. That's really the thing we're fighting. We don't think the Security Department should be a law unto itself."

It was, Betty conceded, a reasonable point of view.

"Argue with Chief Hoyt," she said. "A secret report charged to the print shop is still missing. Mr. Masters sought to impede the search for it; hence he was suspended. What happens to him if the report isn't located, Joel, will be less pleasant."

"Yet he never drew that report from the library! One of his workers did. The fellow quit about a year ago. Why clobber George for a goof committed by someone else?"

"Orders, Joel. The matter was presented to Chief Hoyt. He gave orders; I obeyed them. I'd be very happy to let George off the hook. After all, I'm informally engaged to Luke. But my hands are tied."

"Well, could you soften your written complaint against George?"

"Nope."

"Aw, don't be that way, Miss Sanderson. You're nicer than that."

"But orders are orders, Joel, aren't they?"

His eyes flashed. "It'll be a rugged scrap, Miss Sanderson. Believe me, the Council isn't kidding."

He walked off, and Betty changed her mind about picking up some fiction to read. Instinct told her that the sooner she prepared for the rugged scrap, the better it would be.

11

On the twelfth of August, the Professional Employees' Council formally requested that George Masters be given the week's pay he'd been deprived of. It was also formally requested that the black mark be removed from his record. Betty initialed the memo and sent it by messenger to Chief Hoyt. She then ambled along the hall to the print shop to give the proverbial screw another turn. George greeted her, red faced and gruff. "Miss Sanderson," he asked, "what may I do for you? Shall I call everyone off the job again to look for that silly report?"

"If you will, please," Betty said. "I'll watch this time, if you don't mind."

He turned away contemptuously and went out into the print shop and gave the order. Betty found a chair for herself and watched with what she hoped was a fine display of calm. After a bit, George began to exhibit the old nervousness and impatience. "A grand way to beat the Russians to the moon," he opined. "Let's everybody loaf while the Russians get there first."

"What about dinner on Sunday?" Betty asked. "I have a hired hand now, and you won't know the old ranch."

He smiled terribly. "Dinner with Pru Marshall," he said. "Nice girl, with honey hair and a sweet disposition."

"But you and Luke love me, Pop, so stop being silly."

"Whatever I felt for you was killed when you swung your weight around."

"Well, at least that makes my job here easier. You're on the hook for that report, George. I hate to seem to be a regulation worshiper, but you'll produce that report or wish you had."

"Look, I just obliged a guy who wanted to borrow it."

"The written record doesn't say that."

"You know it," he charged.

"I don't know it," she contradicted.

And of course that was the last straw. Once again George Masters raised an uproar. He called Betty every kind of a sneaking little traitor and actually raised a hand as if to slap her. Several shocked subordinates came running to get between them. Betty sighed, and once again sent a hurry call to Mr. Herman. Mr. Herman came, listened grimly, then led her off to his office. He closed the door, studied her a full minute, then wagged his balding head. "No," he said flatly. "I owe a duty to my self-respect, Miss Sanderson. It's quite apparent to me that you're baiting Masters for some reason I've not been told. I consider that a gross misuse of your position. Please let me say one word more. You've had my department in an uproar almost from the day you came to us over my protest. You have damaged the morale of my group; you have interfered with the discharge of our duties. I won't permit this any longer."

"The report *is* missing, sir, or have you forgotten that? Dr. Schroeder considers it a serious matter."

"There are ways to find a missing report, but your methods suggest you don't know them. Now, then, would you like to transfer out of my department, or must I ask that you be transferred? The only reason I give you a choice, Miss Sanderson, is that you do wear the order of merit."

"You kick me out, sir."

He surprised her. With absolutely no indication of fear, he telephoned Mr. Quigley in her presence and ordered her immediate transfer or else. That brought the industrial relations officer running. Betty sat down and listened while the two men argued the matter. She gave thought to calling her own wheels to come to reinforce her, but then she changed her mind on the grounds that surely a woman her age ought to be able to cope with a tempest in a teapot. When the two fellows had run out of breath, she gave them the benefit of her loveliest smile. "Unofficially," she said to Mr. Harold Herman, "you're ill advised to battle me. I must now charge that Mr. Masters' carelessness with secret material and his lack of self-control make him a very poor security risk. How can you argue that I'm wrong. How can you say to Mr. Abernathy or anyone else that you know more about security matters than my department does?"

"You wouldn't dare!"

Betty said simply, and they were the most difficult words she'd ever uttered: "But I have to dare, sir. I have no choice, you see."

Mr. Herman's nervous swallowing was audible as well as visible. "But if you do that," he said, "you'll smash his career. He can't ever again work for the government or for any organization that handles military contracts."

"Yes, sir," Betty said.

Mr. Harold Herman did a very beautiful thing. "Listen," he said as one human to another, "I beg you to let me handle this. I'll find that report. I'll give Masters such a going-over he'll never lose his temper again. Be reasonable, Miss Sanderson! Masters is a fine man. He has a good record."

"Sorry, sir."

Even Mr. Quigley was startled.

Mr. Herman said: "You butcher! You she-devil butcher, I'll break you!"

And things got warmer . . .

Abner came in the afternoon, troubled. "I hear talk of mutiny," he said. He sat down, dove gray flannels and blue suede shoes with yellow crepe soles. "The complaint seems to be that you're a rough watchdog to have around."

Betty nodded woefully, not liking herself any more than most did these days.

"Have you written the memo?" Abner asked.

"How did you know about it?"

"The whole place knows. Too many witnessed that brawl in the print shop. Also, Herman has contacted the Council and lodged a complaint against you. It's the first time in the history of this division that a department head has sided against a security agent."

"You have to love him for that, don't you?"

Abner shook his head. "I'm not the type to love anyone who gives my girl a bad time."

"You old sentimentalist!"

"Right or wrong, you're my girl."

Betty clasped her hands over her heart and pretended to be on the verge of swooning with rapture.

"But you are wrong, Betty," Abner said seriously.

"What you're doing is making this appear to be a grudge fight with Masters, no holds barred. There's chatter that Luke sees a nurse now, with George's approval. Right?"

"They don't find the report, you see."

Abner gaped.

"How can they?" Betty asked. "They've been through their files a hundred times. The library crew has been through their files. Tech Editorial, Tech Illustration, Graphics, Presentation, Photo Lab . . . every branch and division has gone through its files. No report."

"Must've been put in a burn bag by error."

"No record. I've checked."

Abner whistled.

Suddenly it seemed vital to Betty to make her assignment clear to this fellow who'd said she was his girl, right or wrong though she might be. "Abner," she told him tensely, "the DAGGER III project begins in October. My assignment is nothing less than to tighten security here. The reason for tightening security here is obvious: every scrap of information you scientists develop is processed in Tech Info. What a wonderful place for a spy! Without effort to speak of, he can gain access here in Tech Info to everything developed on this Center. Think of that!"

"Agreed. But . . ."

"Abner, I could show you a list of security violations that would jolt you. Tech Editorial rarely has engineer-authors sign receipt slips when manuscripts are returned to them. The documentary film section borrows from Presentation, and vice versa, at will, and with no record made of the borrowing. Right now there are at least ten classified graphics upstairs in administration, but no record made of that fact. I could go on and on. But that isn't necessary. The fact is that Tech Info under Mr. Herman has grown careless and needs a jolt. George Masters is that jolt. You fire one to save the many and to safeguard vital information."

"But why George, specifically?"

"If a steno is fired, who cares, who worries? Around here, stenos are considered expendable. But if you fire a man of stature, everyone is impressed by your seriousness and becomes careful."

"If they remain here, that is. Right now, there's talk of a walkout by everyone in Tech Info."

"Thanks to Mr. Herman, I dare say."

Abner suggested nervously: "Why not chat with Chief Hoyt, Betty? A walkout might embarrass you, don't you think?"

And things grew even warmer . . .

"Sanderson," Chief Hoyt said, "I don't like to be bothered about these matters. When a girl asks for a department to watchdog, I assume she believes she can handle a department. It's your can to carry, so you carry it."

"But when this whole thing was discussed with you, sir . . ."

"Sanderson, perhaps you misunderstood. I did say I'd back you, but naturally I wasn't promising to back you if you did your work poorly."

"But Fred Teller . . ."

"No, now, Sanderson, don't quote Fred when he isn't here to correct any misquotes. Fred went east yesterday to handle a problem in Louisiana. He won't be back for a month."

"But . . ."

"But what?" he demanded wearily.

"But you did state, sir, that if I made an honest try and failed, you'd not complain."

"Have I complained?"

"No, sir. But . . ."

"If I hear any more buts," he snapped, "I'll get sore. You go back and do your job. For instance, have you written a memo recommending Masters' discharge because he's a poor security risk?"

Betty said she had written it and dispatched it to Herman by messenger.

Chief Hoyt at once picked up the telephone. He requested Mr. Herman's secretary to pick up George Masters' badge and to have George Masters escorted from the premises.

12

THE SUN dropped, the moon rose, and a pleasant chill came into the pine-scented air. Gray Lightning nickered as if impatient to return to the Jolly S. Betty told him crossly to pipe down. The big gray tossed his head and walked off to browse on the sweet grass along the creek. Somewhere in the night a coyote yelped in melancholy fashion at the moon. The wild sounds delighted Betty. Sitting before her little campfire, she wondered why it hadn't occurred to her before to relieve the tension of her work with weekend sojourns in the great outdoors. How soothing the outdoors was, with its colors and shadows, its sounds and its inspiring air. Anxious to enjoy the night to the fullest extent possible, Betty slipped off her boots and wriggled into her sleeping bag. She did not fall asleep, however. Startlingly, a male voice asked: "Lady girl, do you think this is a real smart idea?" While she was struggling to sit up. Duke Elliott came riding into the firelight. Her sputtering protests amused him. "When I hire out," he said. "I hire out. No call to be fussed up, either. Mr. O'Neal pays me pretty good to keep an eye on you as well as the ranch."

"Mr. O'Neal?"

He dismounted and saw to his horse. He then hunkered down before the fire and rolled a cigarette and lighted up. "Lots of folks are bothered about you these days," he confided. "You quitting the corporation?"

"I really don't see what that should concern you one way or another, Duke."

"Well, you take a fellow like me who roams around the rangeland. He gets to see a lot and to hear a lot. It seems to bother folks I appear to have so little to do. They're always offering me work. There's Alice Abernathy at the Wobbly W. There's George Masters. There's Betty Sanderson. There's Mr. O'Neal."

Betty pulled her boots on and joined him at the fire. "Coffee?" she asked. "I have half a pot left. It needs warming, that's all."

"Could be lots of things need warming, lady girl. What good would quitting your job do now?"

"That subject seems to fascinate you," she countered. "I wonder why."

"Well, maybe when you quit I'll apply for your job. Now you take a fellow like me, lady girl. Even with one eye closed, I can shoot the wing off a mosquito at fifty paces. Ride? I tell you, lady girl, if it's got four legs and a place for me to sit on, I can ride anything God ever made. So take that mighty long fence between the Surface-Launch area and the open rangeland. Could be I'd patrol it better than you. A couple of fellows would have little chance to jeep across it to the fence, say."

Betty counted to ten very slowly. She forced a light laugh. "You sound persuasive, Duke. Perhaps I had better refer you to Chief Hoyt, the security officer."

"Is he the fellow who said to me this morning that maybe I better have a chat with lady girl about enemy agents and bullets in the dark tearing into her pretty body when she isn't as alone on the rangeland as she thinks?"

Betty measured the distance between her and the carbine she'd brought along. Too far! She wondered if this fellow knew anything about defending himself against judo. How ridiculous, she thought, for a security agent wearing the order of merit to be caught like this up in the lonely hill country.

Duke Elliott said softly: "Nobody around now, lady girl. George Masters gave it a real good try, but he kept wrestling with old John Barleycorn, and old John sort of wore him down. Last I saw, George Masters was almost home, barely able to stay in the saddle."

The thing to do, Betty decided, was to inch her way toward her carbine. She commenced the inching . . . ambling to the coffee pot, ambling about to find new sticks to refresh the campfire. The technique worked quite well until she was within lunging distance of the carbine. He made her feel foolish after that, however, because just as she was preparing to lunge and grab, he called out: "Field security agent, Miss Sanderson; take a look."

The badge, the card and the letter were the genuine articles. After she'd inspected them, Betty put the coffeepot on and sat down beside him. "So it goes," she said philosophically. "I think I might have reached that carbine, Duke."

"Maybe so, maybe not. Anyhow, it doesn't matter. I used to be a sheriff further north, Miss Sanderson. But the old missile bug got me, and I've been a field security agent ever since. I've never handled a thing like this, though. You ride around and you listen.

You hear a lot of palaver from the hands on the different ranches, but you never hear the one thing you're listening for."

"The fellow who told the reporters how to get to the fence?"

His next words almost made Betty cry. "Nope," they were, "we know that was George Masters. He was fired in New York once for raiding a cash register to buy some John Barleycorn. The reporters threatened to tell the corporation folks about that. Then they convinced him they were just after a story. So George gave them info on the layout of the place inside the fence, then he gave them info on how to get to the fence."

"Shut up!" Betty begged. "Will you shut up?"

He took a handkerchief from his pocket and handed it to her. He investigated the coffee situation while she dabbed at her eyes. "When this is over," he said, his back turned, "you quit, lady girl. You like people too much. If you stay in this work you'll end up in a mental institution. What's wrong with you is that you'll force yourself to do a good job even if you hate doing it. The Chief was plumb worried about you the other day. Said that in his opinion you were near the breaking or quitting point."

"I've always loved Pop, you see."

"He ain't much."

"No one is entirely good or entirely evil!"

"The man hired out to work for national defense. To hide something in his past, he was willing to sell national defense down the river. To me, that sort of fellow is a polecat."

A short time later, Betty returned home, to the astonishment of her mother.

"How come you're back?" she asked. "I thought

you were a tired girl who wanted to be alone for a while."

"Why, I missed you, ma'am. And the great Irisher, of course. Where is he, by the way?"

"Home sulking, I think. We scrapped. He thought we ought to have a surprise wedding and confront you with a *fait accompli* when you came home. I refused. He said I don't love him. I told him not to be silly. He marched off. I think I ought to marry him soon, though. Mr. O'Neal isn't a man who likes to wait."

Betty went to the telephone and dialed the great Irisher's house. He was quite stiff after he recognized her voice, but he came around nicely when she told him she wanted him to dinner tomorrow to meet a young fellow she was beginning to like more and more. "Girl," he said, "always come to O'Neal with your problems. I'm a great believer in family. Now let's discuss this young fellow. It isn't Luke Masters, is it? Fine. I admire Luke. I admire anyone who fights the good fight for his kith and kin. I don't hold it against him that he's hired a lawyer to make you look hasty or foolish. In the same position, I'd do the same thing."

Betty felt a sinking sensation in her stomach.

"When did he do that?" she asked.

"Why, this morning, I suppose. While I was eating lunch, the telephone rang, and it was lawyer Charles Morgan. Charles wanted me to warn you he'd blacken your character if you didn't listen to sweet reason. I told him my fist to his eye would be the result, but Charles just laughed. Why does he hate you? Charles Morgan, I mean."

"High school crush."

"Well?"

"He decided one day that I'd agreed to marry him and was furious when I left for college."

"Is your mother there?"

"Yup."

"Tell your mother O'Neal will hear her apology."

Laughing, Betty relayed the message. About twenty minutes later, the great Irisher was back at the house to demonstrate that all Sanderson problems were now his. He made Betty have coffee alone with him in the kitchen. Over the coffee, his eyes like gimlets, he ordered: "Lass, tell your old man anything and everything you're allowed to tell. This is important. Charles Morgan is no amateur lawyer. I've used him myself, so I know. Have you the right to fire a man as a security risk without a trial?"

"Yes, sir."

"Un-American!"

"No, sir. Working for the government or a defense plant is a privilege, not a right. But don't allow me to give you a false picture of this. While there isn't a formal trial, as such, there are many built-in checks in the system to insure fair play from start to finish. For example, when George Masters was suspended, my request for suspension had to be reviewed by his department head, by the industrial relations officer, and by Mr. Abernathy or his assistant, Mr. Pagano. In each case the reviewers were inclined to side with Mr. Masters. It was only after they were given all the facts that they agreed to suspend him."

"What about this discharge?"

"When a man is deemed by an agent to be a poor security risk, the corporation first removes him from the premises. The full case against the man is reviewed by all the wheels here and then by some of the wheels in New York. If the man's primary crime is just plain human carelessness with classified material, the corporation usually gives him a comparable job in some other area of its activities. The corporation is in many things, sir. They drill for oil. They run huge cattle ranches in South America. They pipe natural gas to many cities in Texas. They have a potash plant in Utah. And if these are just plain business enterprises, as they are, a man guilty of just carelessness would be given work in one of them."

"Then what is he fighting about?"

"His good name, I imagine."

"Why can't O'Neal have a heart-to-heart talk with him and tell him to go work in one of those enterprises?"

"You don't know he'll be offered such a job, you see."

He stiffened. "You mean . . ." he began, and broke off, disturbed.

"All I mean," Betty fibbed, with her fingers crossed childishly, "is that you can't advise him about that until he's been offered a job."

"But they're going to sue you directly!"

"And Charles will be rough, and the employees at the Center will be rough, but what can I do?"

He wagged his head. "Girl," he confessed, "I don't like any of this. And that's the truth, so help me."

"Ah," Betty joshed, "go out and let Mom cheer you up. May I call you Irish Pop, by the way?"

Her sparkling brown eyes and her radiant smile did all the cheering up that was necessary. "That you may, lass." he said. "O'Neal is a lucky man."

13

The lawyer made a difference. Betty felt that difference in the air ten minutes after she had reached her office on Monday morning. Mr. Herman's secretary telephoned there were several large questions concerning the list of security goofs she had left in his possession. Mr. Herman would see her at ten o'clock to discuss them. There was no polite query concerning the convenience of this hour selected by him. Marge Abern made her statements, then broke the connection.

Amused, Betty awaited a visit from Joel Brower, the department's representative on the Professional Employees' Council. He showed up at nine-twenty, jacketless and brusque. "Sanderson," he stated, "we're entitled to a carbon of the discharge request you made. Let's have it."

"Did I hear the word please?"

"You didn't hear the word please. Sanderson, let me level with you. You're the first woman I've met that I despise. You came to this department, swung your weight around, baited a fine fellow unmercifully, then tried to fire him when he lost his temper. I see no difference between your methods and those used by the Gestapo. It'll give me kicks to do to you what you tried to do to George."

Betty rummaged in her file cabinet and found the carbon. She asked him to sign the receipt slip for it, and in his presence placed that slip in the cabinet drawer. Joel read the memo eagerly. His expression underwent a slight change. Betty couldn't resist pointing out to him: "You'll notice, I'm sure, that the charges are quite specific and heavily documented, Mr. Brower. Now I'll admit that the Gestapo sedulously avoided looking for real evidence against anyone, but I'll promise to do better in the future."

"Has the lawyer seen this?" Joel asked.

"Nope. He may have seen Mr. Herman's copy, but not this one. You will have observed, I'm sure, that the memo is classified secret. That's because the name of the missing report is classified secret. I hate to appear a stickler for regulations, but it is a fact that a lawyer not cleared to handle secret material has no right to examine secret material."

His eyes told her he would love to choke her a little.

"Do you seriously believe," he asked, "that George was deliberately careless with that report?"

"My memo speaks for itself, Mr. Brower. And may I point out that you have the right to question me only during a formal hearing authorized by Mr. Abernathy or Dr. Schroeder."

"Come off it, Sanderson. A man's life is being smashed. You could make an effort to be human."

Betty rolled her large brown eyes. "But I never did hear that word please, you see. That will be all, Mr. Brower."

He growled and rushed out into the hall.

Betty counted to five very slowly and then poked her head out into the hall. Yup, the poor guy had goofed! She tooted her police whistle. Joel Brower stopped short. Betty went briskly toward him, wagging her forefinger as at a misbehaving child. Naturally, some other people came out into the hall, so that she had an audience when she declared: "Carrying a secret document in the broad light of day is a security violation, Mr. Brower. Hasn't anyone told you that such documents are supposed to be transported in nontransparent brown envelopes?"

He looked down at the memo, momentarily bewildered.

"In future," Betty said gently, "do obey all security regulations, Mr. Brower."

She continued to make her first tour of the department before her scheduled meeting with Mr. Herman. She nodded cheerfully to this one and that and pretended not to notice some outright snubs she received for her pains. When she presented herself for the interview at ten o'clock, she gave Marge Abern a cheerful nod, too. Marge Abern scowled. "I'll bet you adore pulling wings off flies, Miss Sanderson. Go right in."

Betty went in and nodded cheerfully to Mr. Herman and lawyer Charles Morgan. Charles at least had the grace to rise and hold out his hand. "A long, long time, Betty," Charles said. "I must say you wear well. How is your mother?"

"Fine. She often talks of you, Charles. In fact, she keeps a scrapbook record of your triumphs. She did think you bungled the Peters murder case, but you got Peters acquitted, and Mom is now your ardent fan."

His pale blue eyes twinkled with satisfaction. "One does his best, Betty, and hopes for the best. Now, then, shall we get down to business. I'm very busy these days. And it does seem to me we ought to be able to settle this matter in a few minutes. My client offers his resignation in exchange for an unblemished job history and a reasonably enthusastic recommendation. Mr. Herman agrees to write the recommendation, but he tells me only you can withdraw the charges against Mr. Masters."

"I think you've misunderstood him," Betty said tactfully. "I don't make charges against anyone in the sense you mean. I state whether a person is a good or a poor security risk in my opinion. I provide the authorities an opinion based upon evidence. The authorities then decide whether to retain the person or to discharge him. In other words, Charles, I don't function as a district attorney might, say—adding up the evidence and making charges."

"In other words, then, you will not withdraw the charges against him?"

"Everything is black or white to you, Charles. Unfortunate. I really am here to cooperate in any way I can to insure Mr. Masters is given a fair hearing."

"A report disappeared, you pinned the disappearance on him, and on these grounds informed the authorities that he's a poor security risk? Is it the policy of this corporation to discharge everyone who cannot account for a classified report?"

"A report disappeared; I pinned the disappearance on him. For that reason, and because he impeded me in my efforts to locate the report, I informed the authorities that he's a poor security risk. As for corporation policy: I don't create it. I can't even answer your second question because I don't have the facts in my possession."

"Is there anything else you're not mentioning, Betty? I want you and Mr. Herman to make no mistakes about me. I think I'm a loyal American. Lord knows I try to be. If what you've just told me is the full case against Mr. Masters, I'll work for him and I'll beat you. But if there's more you cannot tell me for security reasons, and if that more is quite serious, then possibly I'll drop the matter here."

"Have you talked to Chief Hoyt, Charles?"

"Not yet."

"Well, there's more. I can't tell you what it is, perhaps he can and will. Why not talk to him?"

It seemed for a moment that his eyes had become little beads of ice. This was not the old Charles, however, who had waxed vitriolic when affairs failed to march as he hoped they would. His forehead crinkled, he murmured something unintelligible, and then he left—presumably to discuss the matter with Chief Hoyt.

Once the door had closed behind the man, Mr. Harold Herman asked: "What else have you against George Masters, Miss Sanderson? Why haven't I been told about it? Is it your hope to embarrass me? Frankly, I fail to understand your attitude."

"I've often wondered about yours, sir," Betty said as frankly. "You were rude my first day here. You deliberately assigned me to the most wretched office you could find. You obviously undercut me, because I had considerable difficulty obtaining even minimal cooperation from your employees. You sought to have me transferred. And all this, Mr. Herman, before you had any opportunity to learn anything about my competence or my personal character. And all this, Mr. Herman, despite the fact that you of all people needed the understanding of a security agent far more than the agent needed yours."

He flushed.

Betty pressed her advantage. "I hired out to do a

job, sir. I consider it an important job, so I'll continue to plug away at it until I'm relieved or transferred. You may make this a personal battle between us, but I won't stop until I've been ordered to stop."

"My sole interest is in maintaining the efficiency of the department and in protecting the interest of my people, Miss Sanderson. I consider that your methods are wrong, that you do more harm than good."

"And you arrived at this conclusion, sir, before I had worked here a day? You're a remarkable man."

The sarcasm stung. "I don't need *you* to tell me how to arrive at conclusions," he said tartly. But in almost the next instant he was trying to pour the proverbial oil onto troubled waters. "My initial displeasure was not with you, Miss Sanderson," he said. "I thought I should have been consulted before you were sent to me. It was my thought that by making things difficult for you, I would express my displeasure to Mr. Quigley and others. A department head must defend his position in the hierarchy, regrettable though that may seem. However, all this is neither here nor there. The fact does remain that you have impaired the efficiency of my people, you have damaged their morale, and that you must go. I will not yield on that point, I assure you."

"Then I have everything to gain and nothing to lose, sir, haven't I?"

"Do your worst," he said calmly.

"As you will, sir. May I have not later than two o'clock a detailed account of the steps you have taken to correct the security problems I listed for you?"

"Oh, I'm ignoring the list, Miss Sanderson. I consider the list outrageous, in fact."

"May I have that in writing, sir?"

"You may not."

"Must I really summon another agent to hear

you say you're ignoring the list of security violations, sir?"

Her brown eyes had never been so steely.

Mr. Herman did some quick thinking. He then called his secretary in and dictated a memo to the effect that he considered the list of security violations to be a spite list developed to protect a young lady who had gone too far in her attempts to justify her continued assignment to his department. The memo was officially delivered to Betty about seven minutes later. Marge even made her sign a slip acknowledging receipt of the memo. And that was her big blunder.

Betty returned to her office and typed a memo of her own to Chief Hoyt. She enclosed a carbon of the list in question, the memo Mr. Herman had dictated. On the basis that it would be foolish to bring a hush-hush project such as the DAGGER III into the department, the departmental attitude considered, she recommended that all information relative to the DAGGER III be withheld from Tech Info until a later date. She dutifully forwarded this memo to Mr. Herman by messenger, and awaited the inevitable explosion.

When the explosion came, she was chatting with an aeronautics engineer new to the base, a handsome golden-haired fellow named Jerome Hogarth. Jerome was full of nonsense about the loneliness of a fellow transferred west, his need for feminine company, the delight he would take in the company of a striking brunette who ought to know better than to become involved with Abner Pritchard, a staid guy definitely beyond thirty.

Mr. Herman's abrupt entrance and choleric face brought the nonsense to an end.

"Miss Sanderson," Mr. Herman declared, "this is war."

Betty said simply: "Yes, sir."

"I demand you withdraw this memo!"

"No, sir."

"Are you insane?" he yelled. "They can't *work* on the DAGGER III without us."

"And they can't work with a department that thinks security regulations are made to be honored in the breach, sir."

"Mr. Abernathy will hear of this, Miss Sanderson."

Betty didn't doubt it. And just then, looking at handsome Jerome Hogarth, she had a great longing for a ride in the wide open spaces, where a girl could be herself and enjoy the life the good Lord had granted her.

14

The red-haired, green-eyed fellow scheduled to be a father in November decided that enough was enough. He gazed out at the October snowfall, the first of the season, and heaved a disconsolate sigh. But having made his decision, he proceeded to activate it. "Chief Hoyt," he said crisply, "return Betty Sanderson to your offices. Give her responsible work, of course. Perhaps you can put her in charge of the security files. But transfer her from Tech Info this afternoon."

Chief Hoyt looked at his assistant, Fred Teller. The silver-haired Fred shook his head. "It would be inadvisable, sir," Fred said to his chief. "Regardless of Herman's squawks, they are tightening up in Tech Info."

"My orders are not to be debated," Cal Abernathy said crisply. "I'm not in the habit of giving orders before I have appraised the situation."

Chief Hoyt took it from there. "Your uncle has given orders also, sir. Whom are we to obey? You can see we're on a tough spot."

"My responsibility, Chief Hoyt."

Chief Hoyt asked doggedly: "May I have a written order, sir? Don't forget I've had personal dealings with your uncle. He might forgive me for obeying a written order from his nephew, but he'd never forgive me if I just took an oral one."

"I hate to do it," Cal Abernathy said. "I know most of the score now, fellows. But big though the DAGGER III project is, it isn't so big we must wreck the Center in order to win the contract. That's what we're doing right now. Herman talks of resigning unless he's given a vote of confidence. The employees are restless. Masters is unemployed, and Lord knows when he'll find a worth-while job. Now to me, the big thing is to preserve the Center intact. We work on dozens of different projects, all of them of value to national defense. Rather than risk successful completion of all those important projects, I'd see to it the DAGGER III was given to one of our competitors."

"Still, sir—"

"George Masters returns to his job. Betty Sanderson is returned to your department. Herman goes it alone with his own security people. If my uncle doesn't buy this, then he gets himself another general manager. Anything else, gentlemen?"

Chief Hoyt barked: "Sir, you've flipped. We can prove George Masters aided and abetted those reporters Sanderson arrested. We can prove security is not what it should be in Tech Info. We can prove—"

"Can you actually prove, gentlemen, that one secret, just one, has ever been smuggled off this center and delivered into enemy hands?"

"Of course not."

Call nodded. "And there, gentlemen, is the other side of the coin. We must take reasonable precautions, yes. But we must not become so cautious that we devote all our attention to security. Our business, after all, is to develop useful information and useful gadgets."

"And sabotage, sir," Chief Hoyt said. "We can prove that, too."

"In Tech Info?"

"Sir, I've told you before that we had two objectives in assigning Sanderson to Tech Info. The first was to correct the security situation there. The second was to convince a certain saboteur that we are concentrating all our attention upon Tech Info for a reason not known to him. The device has worked—perhaps because Betty Sanderson doesn't know she's being used to trap a saboteur. We have good reason to believe that the saboteur has visited her more than once. He had no business in Tech Info, yet there he was."

"Does the girl get killed?" Cal asked. "Rough on a girl who aspires to develop a cattle ranch."

"She hired out as security agent," Chief Hoyt said grimly. "Security agents are expendable."

"Transfer her," Cal said. "You'll get the written order this afternoon. . . ."

When he heard the news, Abner Pritchard gave himself a day off. He drove his Plymouth sedan across the rolling rangeland to the Jolly S. When thumps on the front door of the ranchhouse got him nothing, he ambled about the place until he spotted Betty in the blacksmith shed, shoeing one of her horses. Dumbfounded, Abner sat down to watch. "Are you sure you're a girl?" he asked. "You can perform the most unladylike chores."

"Ranch girls are Jills of all trades, goop. If you hire a man to do everything that needs doing, you run out of cash pronto."

He watched her rasp the left front hoof of the horse. She did it quickly, deftly, and the horse never quivered. A few strokes of the sledge hammered the cherry red shoe into the desired shape. Less than fifteen minutes later the horse was ambling about the pasture off to the left of the barn-red blacksmith shed.

To Abner, the girl in the denim pants and blue denim chore coat was suddenly the most beautiful and knowledgeable girl he'd ever known. He thought he would be the happiest fellow on earth if he could just marry her and help her develop the Jolly S Ranch. He said nothing about this for a time, content to follow her about in the light snowfall and watch her perform odds and ends of chores. When she decided that the newly shod horse had experimented with the shoe long enough, he helped her catch the fellow and put him into one of the comfortable stalls. A suspicion bothered him. "Say," he asked, "these horses don't spend all the long winter here, do they? What a rough life."

"Nope. Right now the idea is to accustom them to the idea of coming home for the night. In a week or so I'll turn them loose to wander as they will. They'll head for Indian Valley, of course, because snow seldom piles up there. But these stalls will be home to them, and they'll head for home each night."

"You have to think of everything, don't you?"

"Or try to remember to think of everything," she said ruefully. "For instance, I forgot to pop the roast into the oven. Mom and Irish Pop will have a fit. Care to dine, to defend me against outraged parents?"

"You know I care to," Abner said softly. "What can I buy, though, to make it a party?"

"Depends upon what we're celebrating."

"Let's say," he said sincerely, "that I'd like to honor a girl who did a difficult job well until the odds against her became fantastic."

Betty was so moved she almost cried. Not if she lived to be a hundred, she thought, would she forget that this man had come at the most difficult time in her life to honor her.

"You're very nice, Abner," she said huskily. She wheeled about to conceal her emotion as best she could. "Nothing to buy," she said. "If you're with family and friends, even moldy old bread makes a party. We have nice homemade bread, though. Why not just bum around for a while? I'll pop the roast in, change, and then we'll talk. You did come to talk, I suppose?"

"Not really," Abner said honestly. "You did your job. Herman finally had you transferred, and you've resigned. Nothing to talk about insofar as the center is concerned. If I could change things for you, I would. But I just run Lab Evaluation."

She nodded and walked off, her very step graceful despite the galoshes she wore. He noticed that with her very step her lustrous brunette hair bobbed prettily over the jacket collar. He noticed also, for some reason, that she walked with remarkably squared shoulders and that she carried her head proudly but not arrogantly. Who and what was she, he wondered, that these little things about her should seem so terribly important and unique? The answer came to him as he swung around to study the vastness of Wyoming in the first snowfall of the season. She was, quite simply, the woman he loved, the woman with whom he hoped to spend the remainder of his life. So although she wasn't particularly special to others, she was to him. And this being so, he thought, how could he let her career at the King Abernathy Missile Test and Development Center be terminated as brutally as it had?

Abner Pritchard made a decision.

Then she got into his car and drove back to Antelope View. . . .

The triumphant lawyer was puzzled when the muscular man with the rich chestnut hair shouldered by him and went into the living room. "You could wait to be invited in," Charles Morgan said. "Trespassing is serious business."

"I'm Abner Pritchard of the Center. I head up the Laboratory Evaluation Department."

"Interesting, but hardly relevant, Mr. Pritchard."

"More relevant, perhaps, is the fact that I intend to marry Betty Sanderson. How many years in jail do I get if I break your nose, Morgan?"

Charles Morgan sat down promptly. "If you blame me for the denouement of the Masters case, you're a fool. The corporation was guilty of hasty action, to say the least. This was demonstrated by the reaction of Mr. Abernathy when I told him that at a public trial he would have to identify every employee the corporation had discharged for careless handling of classified documents. He at once requested my terms and acceded to them."

"Blackmail tactics, Morgan. You're a clever lawyer. You knew darned well such information could hardly be divulged even in a closed courtroom."

"Allow me to correct you. I knew there was little if any such information to divulge. Even cursory investigation and questioning, Mr. Pritchard, revealed that for some reason Mr. George Masters was selected by Betty to be transformed into a horrible example of the fate in store for those who incur the displeasure of the Security Department. The disposition of the case would indicate that the case against George Masters was weak."

"And your insistence that she be transferred from Tech Info?"

Charles Morgan, to his credit, didn't lie. He could have said he had insisted upon a transfer to protect his client from future reprisals. But instead he came out with the flat statement. "Personal satisfaction, Mr. Pritchard. I have no reason to wish Betty well. We dated in high school; I had every reason for believing we'd marry; she reneged. Some take such disappointments well. I don't. I had the opportunity to give her a severe emotional jolt, and I made use of it."

Abner wanted to punch him and then choke him and then kick him. But a better idea occurred to him. "What happens to you professionally," he asked, "when it becomes known that through pressure or blackmail you actually frustrated justifiable attempts to tighten security at the Center?"

"How can it be proved, Mr. Pritchard?"

"I thought I'd hire a lawyer to defend Betty Sanderson. Turnabout is fair play, don't you think? She was given the order of merit for a feat of courage and intelligence. She was given every reason to believe her position in Tech Info was permanent. In the corporation, because of arrangements made with labor, job tenure and job security are guaranteed. Unless, of course, there are security violations. So what you've done, you see, and you a lawyer, is to compel the firm to do something illegal just to satisfy your desire for revenge. I wonder how much legal business you'll get, once these facts are made known."

"Be careful with your accusations, Mr. Pritchard. They could well become legally actionable."

"I'll risk it."

Charles Morgan frowned. He sensed violence coming closer.

"Listen," he said, speaking rapidly, "the situation in that department was impossible. The whole thing was too complex. Something had to give. However, now that Betty has had her jolt, I'll request Mr. Abernathy to return her to the department. But what will be gained? In fact—"

But Charles Morgan never got any farther. Suddenly it seemed that a thousand sirens were screaming in the afternoon. Abner listened in disbelief. But as the sirens rose and fell, rose and fell, it occurred to him that this thing was actually happening, that somehow and in some way security at the Center had been violated so seriously the agents there were sounding a public alarm.

Shivering, Abner rushed out to his car and gunned it across the rangeland to the Center.

15

Betty accepted the emergency summons to walk patrol, knowing little about the reason for the emergency but willing to do what she could. She found it strange, but somehow appropriate, that she should be walking her last patrol where she had walked the memorable one the day she had won the corporation's order of merit. The thickening snow limited her vision, but not dangerously, and as she patiently beat her way to and fro between Gates J and K, she thought it would be even stranger if once again she had to arrest invaders of the Surface-Launch area.

The walkie-talkie gradually gave her the details no one had had time to give her. "Damage confined to lobby of Surface-Launch Building," Elaine reported. Her first instructions, along with more details on the emergency, came about a minute later. "All patrol officers are alerted to apprehend possible saboteur dressed in roughneck red sweater and brown corduroy trousers. Suspect is of medium height, rather slender, and was last seen wearing a blue stocking hat.

Assume armed and dangerous. Repeat. Assume armed and dangerous. Zero procedures authorized. Repeat, zero procedures authorized. One employee injured in bomb explosion that destroyed mockup of DAGGER III in Surface-Launch Building."

What had happened, Betty gradually learned, was that some as yet unidentified person, armed with knowledge of the Center's security methods, had managed to penetrate the Surface-Launch Building, plant a small bomb in the motor component of the DAGGER III mockup, and get out of there before the bomb had exploded. A technician had seen the fellow's receding back, and then the technician had been felled and injured slightly by the explosion.

Puzzled, Betty checked her service revolver and released the safety catch. She wondered what in the world the saboteur had hoped to accomplish by blowing up a dummy display model of the proposed DAGGER III. It was an apparently senseless crime, yet the fellow who had committed it had shown considerable imagination and daring. He had certainly known exactly what he was doing and why he was doing it. But—

"Behold the heroine!" someone said behind her.

Betty whirled.

George Masters grinned tautly. "Just thought I'd come out here to see how you're enjoying a taste of your own medicine."

Betty told him to leave.

George Masters laughed.

Betty warned him that zero procedures had been authorized.

George Masters told her to go ahead and shoot.

At that point, two facts occurred to Betty. The first was that George Masters was quite drunk. The second was that he could hardly have come onto the Center legitimately while he was in that condition.

Sadly, Betty nipped behind him and loped along a few hundred feet. She found the place where he'd managed to dig in under the chain-link fence. Troubled, she went back to George Masters and made the arrest she had to make. "Big heroine," he mumbled, weaving. "What I ought to do is let you go on making a fool out of yourself."

"It isn't even that Luke loves you any more," he said. "To Luke you're dead. Only I can't write people off that way. To me, life is everything. Why do you think I hate this business? Its sole objective is death."

"But why won't you let me make a fool of myself, Pop?"

"I'm not your Pop. I won't ever be your Pop."

Betty switched on her walkie-talkie and made her routine check-in report. Elaine laughed. "You sound as if you're freezing, honey. How come you were silly enough to help out? If I had the Jolly S Ranch and your future, I'd not be risking pneumonia out there."

"The old fire horse heard the alarm."

Elaine chuckled and broke the connection. When Betty returned her revolver to its holster, George Masters nodded. "You're a real strange girl," he said. "You try to break a man because of a silly mistake, yet you don't report him when you catch him in the prohibited area, woozy at that. It's what I've always told Luke. I've always told Luke you're a strange girl. You have to be strange to get into work like this."

Betty asked abruptly: "Who planted the bomb, Pop? Obviously it wasn't you. But you saw the fellow, I'm sure of that. You had to if you crawled under the fence. It would take you at least an hour to work your way across the rangeland unseen. You couldn't have dug your way in easily. Say another hour. All right. The whole thing happened less than an hour and a half ago."

"Abner Pritchard."

"Nasty of him, wasn't it?"

"You know all I ever did do, Betty?"

"Yup. Some reporters who knew your record in New York blackmailed you into helping them try to come up with the newspaper story of the year. Luke inadvertently betrayed your involvement, Pop, when he talked about things he couldn't have known anything about and you couldn't have known anything about unless you were involved. So there's the story behind the needling and behind my recommendation you be dismissed."

He grunted, did George Masters.

"But how could the Corporation tell the full story in court?" Betty asked. "The Corporation would have had to admit its security measures were inadequate at the time, and that admission might have cost the DAGGER III contract. There's been heavy competition for that contract. So you're in and I'm out. But for how long are you in, Pop, unless you redeem yourself?"

"Those reporters are good Americans," George Masters said heatedly. "Do you think I would have helped them if I hadn't known that?"

"I know you wouldn't have helped them had you thought otherwise. Look, Pop. What Herman said one day is true. This is an unpleasant job. But it's a necessary job. I would have had my own mother dismissed in a similar situation. You know that, too."

"All I want is a clear record. I'll quit then and take a job with the local newspaper. But without a clear record, I don't stand a chance."

"I work here, Pop; I don't run the establishment. I'll recommend the bargain to Chief Hoyt, however."

"And if he turns me down and has me jailed?"

A distinct probability, Betty decided. If any benefit were to accrue to poor George, it would have to be shown that he had voluntarily risked his neck to bring the saboteur down . . . and, more, that he had done all this without hope of reward.

"His name, please?" she asked.

He sniffed disdainfully.

"You have to trust me," she said patiently. "If I'm to help you, Pop, you have to trust me."

"Why should I trust you?"

"Because you know that you can. Listen, Pop, I happen to be a woman who fancied herself in love with your son. I knew exactly what it might cost me to needle you and to secure your dismissal. But I had an obligation to the Corporation, to the country, and I did my job. The record says, I think, that I can be trusted to meet my obligation to help you in exchange for information."

The snow thickened, and now visibility did shrink appreciably. Felling chilly, Betty stamped her feet and looked off wistfully at the buildings on her right. All she really had to do to win apologies, reinstatement, promotion, and comfort, she thought, was to report to Elaine in communications that once again she had captured an invader. Chief Hoyt and Fred would do the rest, regardless of what George Masters might believe. Yet how could she do all that to a fellow who'd once begun to build a lovely house for her in one of the beauty spots of Wyoming? Who was she, doggone it, to deny a fellow a chance to redeem himself, to obtain a decent life for himself?

The name, when it came, startled her.

"Jerome Hogarth," George Masters said huskily. "You were wrong about who dug that burrow under the fence. It was Hogarth, not me. What I was doing out there was looking for Duke Elliott. Dirty security agent, stringing me along all the time!"

"How was he dressed?" Betty checked.

"Red sweater, brown pants, blue woolen hat. Not really smart, Hogarth. He was so anxious to get away he never saw me riding along out there in the open."

Again, as once before in the same area, Betty wrestled with her conscience. Should she give an obviously loyal invader a break or not give him a break? This time she decided not to call for reinforcements. She sent George scooting back to his mount on the correct side of the fence, and she moved on along her patrol. When it seemed reasonably certain to her that he'd put distance between himself and the Center, she worked her walkie-talkie again. "Request relief and Fred Teller," she said, "to apprehend the saboteur in conformance with zero procedures."

Elaine lost her poise, for once. "Honey," she gasped, "are you nuts?"

Betty switched off the walkie-talkie and waited. Presently Fred came along, alone, in a patrol car. Fred didn't ask if she were nuts. "The brass almost died," he said happily. "All of Mr. Harold Herman seemed to ooze away after the Chief reported your message. Mr. Calvin Abernathy may still be a redhead when all this is over, but he'll have some gray hairs."

"No relief?" Betty asked, beginning to become keyed up.

Fred met her suspicious eyes. Typically, he gave an honest answer to her unasked question. "The chief and I love your brunette beauty," he said. "We thought we'd like to keep you living a bit longer. You tell me the name, the place, and I'll handle the rest."

"But technically I don't have to follow orders. I came here merely to oblige you."

Fred grinned and waited.

Calmly, Betty got onto the front seat and worked her walkie-talkie again. "Sanderson leaving patrol area with Teller," she reported. "Relief not vital, but technically necessary."

Fred asked: "Is it that important to you, Sanderson? I'll play ball if it's that important."

"To George Masters," she said; "not to me. We pick him up near City Hall. If he performs heroically, he ought to be let off the hook, don't you think?"

"He couldn't ever be cleared again for hush-hush stuff. Certainly not by us."

"A clean record, Fred, and he gets a job with the local newspaper. A mistake is a mistake. He won't make such mistakes again."

"It could be done. There's been a lot going on that we'd like to clear up. If George Masters helps us clear it up, something can be worked out."

That was enough for Betty. She nodded, and Fred drove them out through the guarded gates and along the broad highway to Antelope View. They had to wait a half-hour near City Hall, but George Masters finally came and they proceeded to the Sheldon Arms, in which Jerome Hogarth had his apartment. George's knock brought the handsome aeronautics engineer to the door. George's yell: "You lousy bombing Bolshevik!" precipitated action so rapid that he was smashed flat and Hogarth was running before Fred's reflexes could begin to function. But Betty, at the foot of the stairs, had all the time in the world to aim her revolver at Hogarth's midriff.

Hogarth stopped short, eyes panicky.

"You're under arrest, sir," Betty said mildly. "Do you know what zero procedures means to agents of the Center? It means we shoot first, if necessary, and ask questions afterward."

A terrible thing happened.

"Betty, Betty, Betty," Jerome said chidingly, "this is your lonely engineer, remember? Now why would you shoot a friend?"

He leaped.

Betty just stepped backward.

The poor fellow tried to soften his fall, but he didn't have maneuvering room. Betty heard the crack of a breaking bone just before Jerome Hogarth, saboteur, began to scream in bitter agony.

16

DR. LUKE MASTERS reported somewhat sheepishly that the battered hero was celebrating his heroism in typical fashion back at the house. Betty said quietly that George ought to take the cure, but she didn't embarrass Luke by discussing the matter further. She invited Luke to have coffee and doughnuts in the birch-paneled kitchen of the ranchhouse. The alacrity with which Luke accepted the invitation interested her but left her quite unmoved. "A long time," she commented. "You must let me show you some of the changes Irish Pop is making in this house. In theory, it's now my house. But Irish Pop is the sort of man who's sure he knows better than you exactly how you want your house to look."

"When do they marry?" Luke asked.

"Thanksgiving. We'll have the noble bird for the wedding feast; then they'll fly to Rome. Mom's having a fine time making clothes. Irish Pop is having a fine time buying her clothes. If I suddenly blossom into the best dressed woman in Wyoming, you'll know I

125

inherited either the homemade or store-bought clothes Mom couldn't cram into her suitcases."

Luke added sugar and cream to the coffee. He sat so that he could look out through the uncurtained window at the sparkle of November sunshine on the snow. It was a fine view of approximately a hundred square miles of empty range. A blur on the horizon marked the beginning of the northern mountains. There were clouds over the mountains, as if more snow were being dumped onto them to feed the myriad streams and rivers.

"Dad told me everything," Luke said finally. "Of course I felt abashed. I should have known better than to think you were satisfying some abnormal urge to swing your weight around."

"You should have," Betty agreed. "No matter. The truly important thing is this. I'm now empowered to offer a clean record in exchange for your father's resignation. The mistake will never hinder him in a quest for a job that doesn't require clearance to handle classified matter. He won't ever again be cleared to handle classified matter, however. He must understand that and accept it."

Luke nodded.

"The second condition," Betty told him, "is that your father can never discuss the case with the press. At all times, a carefully worded statement concerning his heroism will be included in all replies to inquiries concerning his record here. The Corporation has no wish to deny him the rewards of his heroism, in other words, but these things are tricky at best and must be handled by authorized Corporation personnel."

Again, Luke nodded.

"There it is in writing," Betty said. "If your father signs the agreement, the unpleasantness is over. I'll then telephone the editor of the newspaper and give George a clean bill of health."

"Almost sounds as if you've made your peace with the Corporation," Luke commented. "Actually, you sound as if you're a junior executive, at least."

Betty grinned but said nothing. Hearing a car coming up the drive, she headed for the hall and front door. The sight of Mr. Herman in the red Thunderbird gave her deep satisfaction, but she did her best to conceal the satisfaction as she stepped outdoors to welcome him to the Jolly S.

Mr. Herman smiled quite jauntily. "My," he exclaimed, "you have a most impressive ranch, Betty. I may call you Betty, mayn't I?"

To put him at ease, Betty said that he might provided he didn't use the liberty as a springboard to a marriage proposal. Mr. Herman laughed and stepped with more genuine confidence from the car. Betty took him into the living room and waved him to her favorite red leather chair near the fieldstone fireplace. She added some sticks and a log to the fire. While he sat enjoying the room and the fire, she nipped out to the kitchen for the coffeepot. "It's my beauty that explains my sudden popularity," she told Luke. "Can you manage alone here for a few minutes? Big business."

He looked at his wristwatch and rose. "I have a few calls to make anyway. Care for dinner this evening?"

Betty conveyed as gently as she could the information that she'd made arrangements already. Luke smiled faintly. "It always happens that way, I dare say. Hindsight may be more accurate than foresight, but it wins you little. I'll have my father sign the document and put it into the mail. When do you need it?"

"Tomorrow, before ten. I'm scheduled to fly to New

York. It appears that the King Abernathy Corporation has several hundred plants and offices scattered about the world, and a Mr. Weatherly, who's in charge of field crews, wants to discuss an important assignment with me."

"But what about the ranch?"

Betty said, not without pride: "They're discussing eighty-five hundred a year plus expenses, Luke. I never dared dream of earning such a salary. With that sort of income, I could stock this place nicely in a few years."

"If you lived. Patients talk to doctors. Hogarth talked to me. His idea, it seems, was to grab you and hold you as hostage while he worked his way out of what he thought was a trap. Fred Teller told me it wouldn't have done him much good. You were all operating under something he called zero procedures, he told me, which meant he'd have shot at Hogarth regardless of the consequences to you. What sort of job is that?"

"Important. If nice boys and men, sailors and soldiers and air force people, can risk their lives every day for their country, why not I? Luke, this is something neither you nor your father has ever really understood about me. I've always considered it a privilege to live in Wyoming, which is another way of saying I've always considered it a privilege to live in the United States of America. Well, I've always thought privileges should be earned to the best of one's ability. You earn it with your work every day, work connected with preservation of life, mitigation of pain and so on. Why not I? And do you know, Luke, we at the missile center are not concerned with death, as your father seemed to believe. Look at nature. In the great outdoors, it's the weak, the helpless, the unwary, the overconfident who are killed. But if you're strong, if you use your intelligence . . . well, it seems to me that if there are godless people in the world intent upon our destruction or subjugation, our best hope for life as we know it is to remain strong. So that's really our concern at the Center: to think and to work so that we can remain strong."

Her glowing eyes silenced him.

"And one thing more," she told him. "If a person is concerned with death rather than with life, he pulls the trigger of the revolver automatically. I could have shot the reporters. I could have shot your father when he stood unarmed and drunk in a prohibited area. As for Hogarth: before a man can leap he must shift his feet. I could have put six bullets into him between the time he shifted his feet and the time he came at me."

Luke inhaled deeply.

Betty saw him to the door, then returned to Mr. Herman. He rose when she entered, and he accepted the offered coffee with a great show of appreciation. "You're a better person than I," he then said in ashamed tones. "I came here partly to tell you that, Betty."

"Quite unnecessary, sir."

"Not to me. I lack your objectivity, I'm afraid. I'm unable to dismiss bullheaded opposition and rudeness as concomitants of life."

"Actually, a department head wouldn't be worth much, would he, if he dumped an employee the instant a charge was made against him? And of course you never did have the full story, just as I never had."

His eyes flashed. "I here and now promise you, Betty, that department heads will be given the full story in future. Much that happened would not have happened had I known everything about George Masters."

"Security measure, sir—"

"No. If I'm considered competent to administer a department charged with vital work, I'm competent to work closely and with discretion with the security agents assigned me."

Betty chuckled; she couldn't help it. "I'm hoping I'm present, sir, when you present that argument to Chief Hoyt."

His manner underwent an abrupt change. "Speaking of that, Betty: naturally, the instant I became informed on everything I requested your return to my department. I pointed out to Calvin Abernathy himself that the details withheld from me were the very details I required all along to assess your work and your character efficiently. Mr. Abernathy was good enough to agree with my contention. He has no objection to returning you to the Technical Information Department if you wish to resume your work there."

It was an appealing proposition. On the basis of her second arrest of a security violator, she would be awarded another promotion that would carry with it a nice salary increase. A girl could live most comfortably on her own ranch if she had an income of seventy-five hundred or so a year. If she were frugal, she could add stock as rangeland was redeveloped. Then, of course, there was the fact that a girl could pick up a social life where she'd left off.

"I'm flying to New York tomorrow, sir, for a chat with Mr. Weatherly. As I understand it, he's second vice president in charge of all field crews and units."

"I know him quite well, Betty. Unofficially, let me tell you that he's a bandit. He allows us to develop talent; then he uses his august position to steal the talent from us. But in his area you'd be just another cog in the national machine. In a sense, even though your pay would be increased substantially, you'd be starting all over again. And you can't always be lucky, you know. You were lucky that George Masters approached you with a deal. You were definitely out, I regret to say, until luck placed him in the position of having something to approach you with. Well, you won't be considered expendable any more. That is, if you remain here. But if you join Weatherly group . . ."

"Or I may remain in retirement," Betty said, although she doubted that. "My future stepfather thinks this ranch could be developed into a paying enterprise."

He was too shrewd. "But you didn't risk your life simply because you wished to retire, Betty. No. You do your work, and it's unpleasant work, because you deem it important. Very well. I can honestly say to you that the DAGGER III project is as important as any other project in all the West. My department does not need a sharper awareness of the need for maintaining very tight security. In my opinion, you're the ideal person to keep everyone aware of the need for very tight security. You've proven your points, all of them. You'll have the complete respect and cooperation of everyone."

With time running short, Betty closed the discussion by pointing out: "Still, sir, I must fly to New York first. I appreciate you having come, though, much more than I can say."

Could he take a hint?

Sure Harold Herman could take a hint. He left three minutes later, giving a girl ample time to take the bath she needed, to do her hair and nails, to dress carefully and effectively, to compose herself before the emotional storm struck.

When the emotional storm struck, however, she found it quite agreeable and downright thrilling.

"You hurry me too much," she told Abner Pritchard. "Why should I say on this particular evening that I'll marry you? Darn it, we've never had many real dates."

"Because if you go to New York, Weatherly will sell you. Weatherly is a born salesman. You're likely to end up in India or some such outlandish place in which we have an office or a plant. It's happened to other career girls your age in this organization."

"Anyway," Betty told him, "I need to think. Abner, be nice! I've been on a security merry-go-round ever since March! I've been following orders without even knowing why the orders were issued. I had to needle a man I've always loved; I had to drop a fellow I thought I loved, I had to battle a department head I really respected. Now I want to relax. How can I relax with you leering at me, or practically?"

He was a good sport, Lord love him. He stopped leering and proposing wedlock and invited her to dance.

17

THE GREAT headquarters building of the King Abernathy Corporation awed Betty Sanderson for all of two minutes. "Mighty overpowering," she told the taxi driver. "We don't even have many mountains in the West as high as that pile of stone."

He liked her easy drawl, her unaffected manner. "Girlie," he said, "you got time to look at some real tall buildings?"

"I have, but the wheels haven't. Life is like that sometimes, I'm afraid."

In the lobby of the great pile of stone, however, Betty discovered to her amusement that she was something of a Corporation celebrity. Hardly had she given her name to the receptionist before the receptionist was holding out her hand and crying excitedly: "Miss Sanderson, can I shake your hand? What a real thrill to meet you! I guess there isn't a girl in the whole place who doesn't wish she were as brave and brainy as you."

So it went, Betty thought gloomily. You could do a fine job for a hundred years and climb very little. But if you were lucky twice, you won not only good promotions but the respect and praise of everyone.

On the fourth floor, in the anteroom of Mr. Weatherly's office, she was asked to pose for a photograph that would be printed in Corporation company newspapers around the world. While she was smiling dutifully, a gross figure of a man came in and stood looking for a time and then snapped his thumb and forefinger. People seemed just to melt away. Mr. Weatherly's secretary said: "Miss Sanderson, may I have the pleasure of presenting Mr. Abernathy? Sir, I'd be very happy to tell Mr. Weatherly that you reached Miss Sanderson first."

"Do so," he requested. He crooked a forefinger, and Betty had to go to the elevator again to shoot further upward through the innards of the great pile of stone. Mr. Abernathy studied her candidly during the ride but said nothing until they had reached his surprisingly small and plainly furnished offiffice.

"You're the type," he said then. "It's peculiar how one type of person gets into one line of work and another type gets into other work. I've noticed that people possessed of quiet faces and steady eyes usually get into some branch of investigative work. Do you aspire to a great career, Miss Sanderson?"

"I've never given it much thought, sir."

"Always an error. Unless you're rich, you should devote all thought to your career. People who claim money is unimportant are idiots. In this country, one of the most enlightened and generous in history, people still die or lead hopeless lives because they lack money."

Betty didn't argue it with him. She suspected he'd be a meaner, sterner adversary than Chief Hoyt or even Mr. Harold Herman.

"Well, Miss Sanderson," he said, "I have given

thought to your career. When I first heard of you, it seemed to me to be intelligent to accomplish a security objective and your downfall at the same time. Your knowledge of the escapade of those newspaper reporters could have been damaging, to say the least. But here you are, a heroine once more, and I never chop off the lucky and the intelligent."

That galled Betty. "Don't you, now?" she asked. "How generous of you, sir!"

He rumbled with laughter. "You remind me of Alice," he said. "She could always snap and snarl, too. Well, I permit you to snap and snarl. But just you remember this. My first duty, now and always, is to my country and to the sixty-odd thousand who work in this organization. I won't give you details, but let me say this. It was nip and tuck to get the DAGGER III contract. Had word of the reporters' escapade reached the press, the contract would have been lost. The right people were aware of our sabotage problem, you see. That, plus the near success of the reporters, would have cost us heavily."

"It ought to be assumed, though, that security agents do know how to keep quiet."

"Assumptions are a luxury few people can afford, Miss Sanderson. No matter. There you are. You have intelligence, spirit, dogged determination. Most of all, you have luck. We can use you here in headquarters. By that I mean, you would undertake roving assignments for me personally, assignments involving courier services, security checks, and the like. Interested?"

Betty eyed him, flabbergasted.

"Or here's another proposition," he said. "My nephew informs me there's good money in cattle. Now I happen to know that, because we own great ranches in Latin America. Still, we have no cattle holdings in this country, and I understand there's much range to be had in Wyoming for relatively little. Assume we begin with the Jolly S. To it we add all the rangeland adjacent to the Center. We stock the ranch, we operate it efficiently. A profitable venture, do you suppose?"

"Yes, sir."

"Why?"

"Obviously, sir, even if you never sold a pound of beef, you could charge the losses to the Center and make money through tax savings on the profitable operations there."

His shaggy brows lifted. "I expected that," he said. "Your professors inform me you showed promise in business administration, your university major. Why did you get into security work?"

"It paid higher wages, sir."

"No other reason?"

"Well, someone does have to do that work, sir."

"I wonder. I think that if you operated under the general direction of my nephew you might become a good manager of that ranch I was talking about. Well, it's the same pay for either job—nine thousand a year and reasonable expenses. Which job will you take?"

Betty smiled, realizing in that moment that the objective here wasn't to find a brilliant worker for a particular job but, rather, to find a particular job for a worker the Corporation had had to use somewhat shabbily.

"Housewife," she said, hoping Mr. Abernathy would understand.

He looked puzzled. "The doctor? But I was told by Mr. Quigley that we had cost you your doctor."

"I think the director of the Lab Evaluation Department, sir."

"Think?"

Then her blushing cheeks, her embarrassed eyes attracted his notice and amused him. He laughed. "Oh, of course," he said. "All along it was one fellow; then the other fellow came along. Now you're confused because you don't think you're the type to be swept off your feet in a split-second. Rubbish. Well, none of my affairs. I'm a businessman. Sometimes, it's true, I allow the human element in a situation to distract me from profit-making, but not often. I did believe, Miss Sanderson, that we owed you a great deal for obedience to orders that must have puzzled you and even troubled you. Too many little things were happening out there for all the malfunctions of equipment to be accidental. Then the reporters penetrated the heavy security area, and that could not have been accidental, either. So it seemed intelligent to the directors to select a particular department in which to raise a security furore. It was thought, as you've probably guessed, that the saboteur would mistakenly conclude there was something especially hush-hush in Tech Info, and that he would one day blunder into a trap. Hogarth almost did, you may as well know now. One of our undercover agents actually spotted him in Tech Info after hours. The objective of the bombing, Miss Sanderson, was to compel us to shift our attention to the Surface-Launch area. Hogarth then intended to rifle your file cabinet for the hush-hush material."

"But why?"

"People have sold their countries down the river before, Miss Sanderson. A pity, but there it is. By the way, we intend to insure that the publicity in this matter will be limited. A simple statement will be made concerning the bombing and the apprehension of the bomber. It will be said that the man's capture was effected by George Masters and an unidentified security agent. Agreeable?"

"Certainly, sir."

"Until you become a housewife, what do you wish to do?"

"Tech Info, sir?"

"All right. Now to make amends. We have an excess of registered stock on the Wobbly W, I understand. My nephew will deliver a hundred head to you in the spring. Also, if you wish to lease certain grazing rights for a period, contact my nephew."

Betty inhaled deeply.

This, then, was how one of your dreams came true? Fantastic!

And yet, wonderfully, it was true. Hardly had she returned to the Jolly S the next afternoon before the Wobbly W foreman came driving up in a red pickup truck. "Tim Horton," he introduced himself. "The boss man says we're holdin' some stock for you. It would sort of help us keep an eye on them if you was to come point out which is yours."

"You want my mother, then, Tim. Mom has a much better eye for stock."

Betty loped up to the bedroom. Her mother said she was much too busy to bother about smelly old things like cattle. However, she changed her tune when Betty had given her the full story. "I'd better handle this," Hazel said crisply. "Your father always claimed a ranch is no better than the quality of its stock. You don't want a million head here, either. Stick to quality, and the ranch will be a paying proposition."

After her mother had left, Betty concluded the remaining business. She telephoned Chief Hoyt and told him she was again on the payroll and permanently assigned to watchdog Tech Info. Chief Hoyt chuckled. "Sanderson," he said, "who do you think sent Herman to you in the first place? Why, you're a natural for Tech Info. You'd never have gone there in the first place if I hadn't known that. You can read, Sanderson. It isn't every person who knows how to read, now is it?"

He switched her call to Mr. Herman's office. Betty told him of the arrangements made with King Abernathy, and Mr. Herman sighed a bit wistfully. "I have never met the man," he said. "I'm happy to have the assurance that a Mr. King Abernathy exists. Needless to say, Miss Betty Sanderson, I'm happy to have you back again. What about dinner some time soon? I hope to prove I'm not really the ogre you must think me."

"I never did think it, sir. Any time after this evening will be fine."

The last call, she discovered, was unnecessary. As she was asking to be switched to Lab Evaluation, the doorbell rang. It was Abner, all right, dressed in slightly grease-stained coveralls. "Fiddling around with a new missile hoist," he explained. "I don't know why I do these things, but I do."

"What about dinner?" Betty asked promptly. "We have all sorts of nice things in the house."

"Fine."

Betty went outdoors and walked him around the house the better to point out Jolly S property. "We own out to that butte," she said. "Mom's out looking over some prize stock Mr. Abernathy has given me for some reason or other. Know anything about a ranch, Abner?"

"I specialize in ranch girls," he joshed. "I fall in love with them, and after that I can think of nothing else."

"But you don't really know me, do you?"

Abner chuckled and swung her around to face him. "There you are," he said. "What else must I know? And I may as well tell you that Mr. King Abernathy himself has sent me a telegram of congratulations."

Betty gasped.

And that was the last sound she could utter for a

full minute. For at that moment Abner decided her lips really ought not to be ignored and took her into his arms.

Betty was scandalized. Didn't he know that a security agent had a reputation to protect?

"Regulation 190 forbids security agents to make public spectacles of themselves," she told him.

But Abner had the answer to that. He pointed around at the vast range, the distant mountains, the great sweeping blue skies of Wyoming. "Who's to see?" he asked. "Or do antelopes count?"

Betty spotted the inquisitive antelope and yelled for it to scat. The antelope did scat.

"Definitely," she told Abner Pritchard, "antelopes don't count."

THE END

Belmont Romance Books

USE SPECIAL ORDER FORM ON LAST PAGE
TO PURCHASE THESE NEW BELMONT BOOKS

☐ **LOVE IS ENOUGH,** by Peggy Gaddis
Two men came into Jill Barclay's lonely life—one to bring happiness and the
other to destroy it.   #92-634, 50¢

☐ **BEYOND THE CLOUDS,** by Delphina McCarthy
Pretty Pat Aylmer found excitement in international flying—and disappointment
in shattered dreams.   #92-635, 50¢

☐ **PEACOCK HILL,** by Peggy Gaddis
The story of a young woman who became a widow one hour after her marriage
and the strange secret which haunted her.   #B50-637, 50¢

☐ **THE LOVING HEART,** by Joan Garrison
Lovely Doris Scott was captured—and enraptured—by a double involvement.
                                                                  #B50-638, 50¢

☐ **THE PERSISTENT SUITOR,** by Peggy Gaddis
The Bentley sisters came to their secluded island paradise to forget their bitter
disappointments in love. *But they were not alone.*   #B50-649, 50¢

☐ **ESCAPE FROM LOVE,** by Betty Blocklinger
The tender story of a woman who was unable to face love until she had the
chance to escape from it.   #B50-650, 50¢

☐ **NURSE BY NIGHT,** by Doris Knight
A nurse in love with a doctor is not unusual, but Norma and Tony were unusual
people . . .   #B45-902, 45¢

☐ **THE JOYOUS HILLS,** by Peggy Gaddis
A big city career girl seeks solitude in the Joyous Hills, but finds something
else . . .   #B50-653, 50¢

☐ **SNATCH A DREAM,** by Joan Garrison
Life holds such a great promise . . . but Mary felt trapped in a small town,
forced to run a small business.   #B50-654, 50¢

☐ **WAIT FOR THE DAY,** by Marguerite Nelson
She was engaged to Brad, but she knew she was losing him . . . slowly but
inevitably.   #B50-658, 50¢

☐ **BELOVED INTRUDER,** by Peggy Gaddis
Joyce Hilliard was a New York girl in love with an Atlanta man, but when she
went to Atlanta to marry him she found herself an intruder in what would be
her own home.   #B50-659, 50¢

☐ **COME INTO MY HEART,** by Peggy Gaddis
A practical joke catapulted Kerry Martens into a deep conflict—which of the
two Waterman brothers could she really be happy with?   #B50-665, 50¢

☐ **READY TO LOVE,** by Jeanne Bowman
She had been too busy for love—now she feared love was not ready for *her.*
                                                                  #B50-666, 50¢

☐ **A LITTLE LOVE,** by Peggy Gaddis
The wedding plans were made, but Kelcy's bridegroom eloped with the maid
of honor . . .   #B50-671, 50¢

☐ **CLOVER HILL,** by Ethel Bangert
A four-sided triangle brought complications too difficult for young Julie Bond.
                                                                  #B50-672, 50¢

☐ **HOMECOMING,** by Adeline McElfresh
Ann Merick returned from her vacation to find her best friend married to her
sweetheart.   #B50-660, 50¢

☐ **WHERE LOVE IS,** by Peggy Gaddis
A carefree young woman is forced to decide between the two men who love her.
                                                                  #B50-661, 50¢

☐ **REHEARSAL FOR A WEDDING,** by Peggy Gaddis
She was determined to achieve security, even if it meant stealing her best
friend's childhood sweetheart.   #B50-673, 50¢

☐ **A TIME FOR STRENGTH**, Nell Marr Dean
Dr. Janice Stanford was at the crossroads of the most important decision of her young life. #B50-677, 50¢

☐ **ROBIN**, Peggy Gaddis
The girl was young, attractive and ready for life—but romance was to be denied her. #B50-678, 50¢

☐ **GOLDEN RAIN**, Irene Roberts
All was bleak and hopeless until a charming young playwright walked into Carol's life. #B50-679, 50¢

☐ **SHATTERED HALO**, by Adeline McElfresh
A young woman's certainty about love—and life—was shattered by a series of anonymous telephone calls. #B50-674, 50¢

☐ **WEDDING SONG**, Peggy Gaddis
Through the veil of overburdening problems Nora sees a new life, a new love—and a new enchantment. #B50-684, 50¢

☐ **THE QUESTING HEART**, Joan Garrison
Little did she dream that her devotion to duty would place in jeopardy her devotion to the man she loved. #B50-685, 50¢

Romantic Suspense Novels

☐ **THE STARVED**, by Arthur Thompson
An extraordinary novel of a woman born in sorrow, in love with a man she doesn't know. #92-616, 50¢

☐ **DOORS TO DEATH**, by Lee Crosby
What was the mystery of Crane Mansion? A secret so horrible that neither love nor death could reveal it. #B50-629, 50¢

☐ **SHADOWS ON THE WALL**, by Mary Reisner
Death visited the huge Victorian house, perhaps he had come to stay . . .
#B50-641, 50¢

☐ **THE SECRET OF KENSINGTON MANOR**, by Genevieve St. John
Why did Lori Kensington have to come here to die? Or was it to find love . . . ?
#B60-053, 60¢

☐ **BRIDGE HOUSE**, by Lee Crosby
Would love be enough? Could a woman's faith and trust unlock the terrible secret of Bridge House? #B50-644, 50¢

☐ **HOUSE OF COBWEBS**, by Mary Reisner
The House of Cobwebs is a trap spun maliciously for Serena and the man she loved. Could they escape with their lives—and their love? #B60-052, 60¢

☐ **HOUSE OF DISTANT VOICES**, by Evelyn Bond
How could anyone know what she was going through, when she herself wasn't certain? #B50-662, 50¢

☐ **THE DARK WATCH**, by Genevieve St. John
She was proud and proper—but she loved a man with a fierce temper.
#B50-667, 50¢

☐ **THE SHADOW ON SPANISH SWAMP**, by Genevieve St. John
She had been warned, but she refused to believe she was a bride of Death.
#B50-669, 50¢

☐ **THE VICTORIAN CROWN**, by Edwina Noone
Her only hope for romance—or even life—lay in The Victorian Crown.
#B50-675, 50¢

☐ **THE HOUSE ON CABRA**, June Wetherell
She shuddered in fear from every footstep, for danger—even violent death—lurked in every corner of the old Bath House. #B50-681, 50¢
